TREACHERY ON OKALOOSA ISLAND

The Sequel to

DEATH DOESN'T VACATION
ON OKALOOSA ISLAND

remembering

Joyce

The world and its desires pass away, but
whoever does the will of God lives forever.

GEORGE D. KING

authorHOUSE®

AuthorHouse™
1663 Liberty Drive
Bloomington, IN 47403
www.authorhouse.com
Phone: 1 (800) 839-8640

Published by AuthorHouse   01/26/2016

ISBN: 978-1-5049-7379-3 (sc)
ISBN: 978-1-5049-7378-6 (hc)
ISBN: 978-1-5049-7380-9 (e)

Library of Congress Control Number: 2016901000

Print information available on the last page.

Any people depicted in stock imagery provided by Thinkstock are models, and such images are being used for illustrative purposes only. Certain stock imagery © Thinkstock.

This book is printed on acid-free paper.

Treachery on Okaloosa Island

and

Death Doesn't Vacation on Okaloosa Island

have their own Face Book pages where I post pictures of
the setting, updates, and how to obtain the books.

Thank you to all the people who
contributed to this and helped
to get it published

The characters in this novel are totally fictional—made-up from my
imagination. Some of them have characteristics of people I actually know
but I certainly don't intend my fictional ones to represent those people. A
great part of the setting will be familiar to some readers but many places
have been altered or created by me in places where they don't exist. As far
as I know, none of the happenings of this work of fiction have ever occurred
on the Panhandle of Florida nor anywhere else for that matter.

Setting the Stage

"Haw!" "Haw!" "Haw!"

I look down toward the beach to see if Jonathan L is sitting on the volleyball goal post but he isn't. Then I realize there are no gulls flying on our beach at all. A harsh hullabaloo starts over on the roof of the Dolphin building which forms a big V with my building opening out toward the beach. I physically shudder because I see the roof is lined with crows.

To top that, they are sitting silently waiting for something to happen it seems. Oh God I think, do they foretell another horror like that day a year ago last June when they had gathered on the low white perimeter wall that surrounds the La Mancha property? I remember they gathered into a huge swirling flock and flew as one out over the Gulf.

A group of crows is called 'a *murder* of crows' and this group had death on its mind. They never fly far out from the beach, as they seem to have an aversion to being over a big stretch of water. They just never do that and yet they went out that day so far they were only black specks as I looked at them. Then they headed back in a flurry of squawking and shrieking and lined up on the wall and on the roof of the gazebo looking out into the water. Fights broke out among them and I saw one nearly killed by three others.

Crows don't sit in a line and all watch the same direction, but they did that day.

It was just an hour later that Josephine Jones's body washed up causing the many tourists on the beach to scatter like sand crabs; Josephine was the second body to land on our beach last summer.

Now the crows are back--lined-up again like sentinels on the Dolphin's roof. As if they know I see them, they begin cawing madly, but the harsh caws sound like the first letter is an 'H.' Just an old man's imaginings, I try to laugh at myself, but it sounded like they were all laughing. Were they warning that we are in for a summer like last year's?

Haw! Haw! Haw!

Almost like synchronized divers, they peeled off the roof starting at one end until they are were flying in an almost perfect circle with stragglers flying in and out, between the Dolphin and my building, the Pelican. They usually fly in silence and start their cawing when they reach a perch, but not this time—they were shrieking their 'Haws' as they flew. Then a leader pulled out of the circle to be followed one-by-one by the others as they flew out of view inland away from the Gulf.

I will not see them again during the rest of the trial, but their visit put some words in my mind that meant much, "Fasten your seat belts, Boys. It's going to be a bumpy ride."

1

Going to be a bumpy ride...

"TWELVE? NO! There are not twelve. Twelve is a good number, a Holy number. Count them again, you heathens! For there are not twelve of them," raged the almost clown-like figure as he exited the elevator on the sixth floor porch where we were all sitting in an assortment of chairs looking out over the Air Command's fence at the nesting place of the green sea turtles.

Like a prophet of biblical days, he stood waving the gnarled wooden staff he carries, "No, NOT Twelve! Even the Evil One himself would not let there be twelve of them out there in that pit of Sheol… that wilderness where they lurk in hiding…"

I almost burst out laughing as The Reverend Levi Crabtree approached us there on the sixth floor porch of Sea Turtle building. He waved his staff, a piece of hickory hardened and bent into what could easily pass for a shepherd's staff in a Christmas pageant except it was much shorter.

"Count them again! For there are not twelve of them. There must not be twelve." He strutted back and forth more like the leader in a New Orleans funeral march, I thought, than a prophet leading his flock to enlightenment.

Reverend Levi Crabtree appeared at the La Mancha last fall, along with the three women who are with him, and purchased two condos on the sixth floor of my building, the Pelican, and since then has been somewhat of a rude diversion to our daily lives.

The mother turtle returns to the Air Command's sand each year for that is where she was hatched. She lays her catch of eggs so inconspicuously that a common person might never find her nest, and there are many, many of the hatchlings for when they hatch they must make the perilous trip to the water.

The herons knew some turtle eggs were getting ready to hatch. We had counted the herons who stood like statues hiding behind as little as a stalk of sea oats. They didn't make a movement but watching them through my binoculars, I saw an eye dart back and forth now and then as there was movement in the sand where the little turtles were breaking out of their nest. I wondered why the herons even bothered to 'hide' as the turtles surely could not see them; some primitive hunting trait, I guess.

The Reverend was acting the Old Testament roll of prophet filled with wrath because we had counted loudly that there were twelve large herons hiding in the sea oats or low scrub brush out among the hatching nests. Each year as the sand stirs and shifts and the little turtles rake their way to the surface, there is a mass killing of the tiny four or five ounce babies. They sometimes have hundreds of yards of sand to go through to get to the water and even then, a fish might be waiting for a little meal.

The twelve herons were waiting to ambush them.

We've turned the affair in a macabre sort of party as we gather with Don and Shirley Herd and Diana and Barry Page who live side-by-side on the sixth floor of the Sea Turtle to watch the frantic journey to the Gulf on our left or to the Sound on our right. Shirley is known for her chocolate chip cookies and delicious carrot cake so we sit drinking lemonade and eating cookies and carrot cake as the herons prepare to have their feast.

"Count them again, I say! There must not be twelve," he shouted.

Who was this weird little man? He is barely five feet tall, can't possible weigh a hundred pounds, has sandy red hair that hangs limply toward his shoulders beneath the grey battered felt hat he always wears, and almost spits as he shouts out his words. As I looked at him standing there, the herons came to mind as I noticed his piercing eyes that darted from side to side seeing everything around him and his long sharp nose that looked as if it had been broken. I almost laughed aloud as I thought maybe someone had heard just a little too much from this strange little man and had clobbered him on his nose. For such a little man, his voice is deep and loud and frightful at times; the only comparison I can think of is Bicycle Bob's loud rowdy laugh, but Bob's is not frightful. Crabtree's light complexion certainly doesn't fit in with the lack of shade at the La Mancha so freckles the color of his hair seemed to cover his little short arms and his too wide forehead.

Walkin Al starts calling out pointing to where one of the herons is and those of us with binoculars start calling out "there's one" and "there's another." Bicycle Bob's loud shouts drown out the rest of us, "There's number nine right there by the fence." This time we count thirteen and the Reverend is satisfied.

"That is an Evil Place, a place of the Wilderness, a place that God cleanses frequently with great Winds," he jabs his staff in the direction of the nests--four or five quick jabs. "It is a place where no one travels on foot, a place where that island," as he points to Egg Island out in the Sound, "has fallen from the realms of the heavens where it splatted—landed like a broken egg—to slow down the commerce of man. Soon that island will be a place of shadow, a hidden place, a Glass not Seen Through!" And with that he left us, poked the elevator button with the end of his staff, and disappeared into the open door.

We were laughing, some of us with tears running down our cheeks, before he got down to the fourth floor.

Don, who is a very sharp octogenarian quipped, "Someone could have pushed him over the rail."

Walkin Al, who may be the most serious of our group, said, "God's Prophet in bib overalls and black patent leather shoes. Wonder if his staff turns into a snake?"

We all laughed and since the sun was sinking into the Gulf, we said our goodbyes, gathered up our own chairs, and headed to our various condos.

Since Shirley thinks I am an old man who can't take of himself, I left with a bag of chocolate chip cookies and two large pieces of carrot cake. She is the prime example of a pampering mother, and when she and Don take their afternoon strolls down to the gazebo and around the property, I am reminded of gentler days as they hark back to characters straight from Jane Austen or some other Victorian soap opera.

But Crabtree is at the La Mancha and as I take the elevator to my third floor condo in the Pelican, I wonder if he's just a kooky weird little blow hard, or if he might be a distraction to keep us from noticing what is happening around us? Everyone at the La Mancha knows I 'see' too much in things especially after living through the events of last summer and I laugh at myself and get ready for bed.

2

Getting Involved

The next morning as I slide the door to my balcony open and step out, I glance at the big green and blue coffee mug in my hand that has a spiny lobster on it. Some of my students in Albuquerque gave me that mug long ago—long before I even considered retiring to the Panhandle of Florida. Remarkably, it is almost the same emerald green as the Gulf I stand looking at this beautiful morning with pink and orange tinted clouds filling the sky as the sun rises east of us over at Destin.

From my third floor balcony I can see the reconstructed gazebo and the big Y shaped pool that Brantley had almost destroyed a little over a year ago when he crashed his helicopter into them. Poor Brantley was controlled by two worlds and could not live in either of them. Thankfully, I never knew his mother, but she must have been what the Reverend Levi Crabtree would call 'pure evil.' She had made Brantley's life a hell and he had accidently killed her. But that fact was something none of us would ever prove—that had died with him as he deliberately crashed that copter into three palm trees and the La Mancha gazebo and pool.

Those of us at the La Mancha were surprised when we found out that Marvin was really a DEA officer and not the Grounds and Building Foreman at the La Mancha as he pretended to be. I had suspected he was not what we had thought long before the others because of being caught up in the investigation that Marvin and J C Blevins were conducting concerning Launie Sanderson. I suppose the only other person who knew about Marvin was Bette, the La Mancha Manager.

Marvin returned the other day and was in the courtroom. He grinned that ear-to-ear grin of his at me across the room but he left the courtroom sometime during the proceedings so I never got to talk with him.

He still lives a few miles west of Fort Walton Beach just off Highway 98, but we seldom see or hear about him. I did hear he had been sent down to Miami on another mission to search out the drug dealers who bring so many drugs into the Panhandle. It never occurred to me before Launie shot Ollie that drugs are so prevalent in our part of Florida.

Of course, she had the perfect front for selling them—or whoever she worked for had created the perfect front. Cars with license plates from almost every state parked in front of *Launie's Gentlemen's Library,* which we all thought was just another strip joint, or 'something a little more' as Bicycle Bob would loudly and crudely shout and then laugh his boisterous laugh. With over three million tourists in our area each summer, those out-of-state plates were never suspect.

After she was arrested for killing Ollie, we would sit around the reconstructed big Y pool and talk about how she had almost escaped. Prosecuting Attorney Curtis Porter would have a hard time convicting her if it weren't for the witnesses who would testify they saw her shoot Ollie, drag him to the back of the *Lollipop,* her big blue and white yacht, handcuff his body to two five gallon plastic buckets of paint, and struggle to push him and the buckets off the back of the yacht.

H. Russell deLong, the owner and patriarch of the *NorthWest Daily,* had hired me to write the stories about the happenings at the La Mancha after that first body had washed up on our beach. My condo in Pelican building was a front row seat to most of the events.

My firsthand knowledge of what had happened when Brantley had completely lost his mind and finally crashed his helicopter a few yards below my balcony destroying the gazebo and the pool itself and when the body of Brantley's mother was found hanging in the wardrobe in their condo led him to ask me to write for the paper. Those events had nothing to do with Launie, but when she sent Ollie to retrieve that package from our beach and when Josephine Jones's little Corgi, Skipper, had been

6

attacked by some maniac with arrows shooting both Skipper and me, I became involved with Launie's story. My articles appeared in the paper for several weeks as I wrote them in serial installments to increase the paper's subscriptions.

Because of the popularity of those stories, H. Russell hired me to be in Judge Jeffrey Bickel's courtroom during Launie's trial. I have a Press Badge and a reserved seat behind the railing that crosses the courtroom dividing the spectators from the defense and prosecution tables.

I was pleased that my friend, Bicycle Bob, was there every day sitting right beside me, but wondered how he got a pass day after day. Bob had been in court every day since it started months ago except on Wednesdays when he went fishing out in the Gulf. One of his luxuries is his fishing boat, the *Choctaw Pride*, which he bought with money he got from his parents. Bob is a native of Fort Walton Beach and knows 'everyone worth knowing' in Okaloosa County, so he's a great help to me. He lives in Sea Shell Building at the La Mancha on the fourth floor with a view of the Sound and the new jail on the other side.

I welcome Bob's hearty laughter and banter as we sat through the long days and it's pleasant to have lunch with someone I really like. His presence at lunch probably stops many curious people from coming by my table to quiz me about what I will write for the paper the next day.

I grew tired of having to be there every day and having to find out each night if court would be in session the next day for it had been going on for about six months. Nothing worth writing about had happened by this time as it took weeks for the two sides to agree on a jury and Matt Schaberg, Launie's lawyer, had argued point after tiny point about what I thought were nonsensical things. He had wanted the trial changed to another venue, he argued that Judge Bickel should be replaced abut finally shut his mouth about that when he learned Bickel would be the judge in any venue in Okaloosa County, he wanted the jury after it had been seated to take a trip to the place the murder was supposed to have happened and Bickel had finally allowed that. That trip in three pontoon boats—one filled with lunch and drinks for the twenty or so people on the trip, must have cost Okaloosa County several thousand dollars and had taken almost a month to plan and get everything together to do on the three mile trip west on the Sound. It had not value at all for the silt, debris, and tides had completely changed the landscape there and all that could be seen was just another stretch of the Sound and where the Black Drainage Ditch enters the Sound.

Had I known what was going to happen in that courtroom, I would never have agreed to do it.

And yesterday, I saw the crows....

3

"she'll throw you like a dice...."

I don't remember seeing Launie Sanderson but two times and what walked into the courtroom that first morning was not what I remember seeing.

I had the habit of walking up Santa Rosa Blvd to the 'Thumb' as all the beach attendants call the quick-stop store about a mile from the entrance to the La Mancha. I remember that morning almost two years ago like it was yesterday. I was in a hundred yards of so from my goal of getting a fruit pop at the store when I saw this bizarre figure approaching me. She was wearing high heels, as high as I have ever seen, with voluminous pants that clutched in at her thick thighs and a flimsy blouse that strained to cover her massive bosom. Her face caused me to think of a clown as she had thick make-up in various shades plastered from neck line to hairline.

I thought of my favorite actress of all time—Bette Davis. I regret that I thought of her when she portrayed an ugly old-maid who was living in guilt because she had been lied to about hurting her sister when they both had been upcoming figures in vaudeville. I suppose this all came to mind because Launie had escaped reality with drugs and Davis' character had escaped reality by living in the past as her prize possession was her Baby Jane doll.

But, it was Davis' hideous face coated almost white with a painted-on beauty mark that I remember most. And here coming toward me in real life was that apparition walking down the running path. I almost turned and went back home because I didn't want to pass her on the path, but then she stopped and looked at the upper floor of one of the tallest condo complexes on the Island and then she turned and walked back the way she

9

had come. Her wobbling rear end must have been as wide across as 'two axe handles' as my granddad used to say and her butt halves were like two pigs fighting each other in a sack.

I had no idea then but it was Launie Sanderson who I almost had to meet there on the walk.

I did see her again one day shortly before we all read about Ollie's death in the *NorthWest Daily*. I was in High Tide which is the wonderful seafood restaurant at the end of the Blvd at Highway 98. I eat my lunch there often and was late that day. At about three o'clock I guess, as I was finishing an oyster Po' Boy, she walked in.

All the usual noise and banter from the friendly waitresses stopped and for a moment there was almost silence in the place. Launie stood there with a blouse which was stained all the way down her fat sides from sweat coming from her arm pits. Her face was covered with the same stinking sweat so she grabbed a big hand full of napkins from the pile on the bar and starting mopping her face. She caused the make-up to smear in several places as I heard her order crab claws to go.

As she stood there waiting for her order, Celeste, one of High Tide's friendliest waitresses brought her a tall glass of water. I saw Launie's face as she turned toward Celeste and realized that Launie was so high on some kind of drugs that she probably didn't know where she was.

Celeste also brought Launie her crab claws. I saw her pull a bill from the fat wallet she took from the bag she was carrying, put it on the counter and start for the door. We all watched as she first bumped a table, let out a string of cuss words, and then had a lot of trouble getting the front door open. We could see through the front window as her new bright green Caddie squealed out of the parking lot and into the traffic. It raced across Highway 98 and around the corner toward her place.

"Do you believe that? She almost caused a wreck out there too. My God, she's left a $50 bill! Glad I was persuaded to wait on her."

After all the 'wasted' time as far as I was concerned, the trial would actually become a reality this morning in Judge Jeffery Bickel's courtroom.

The woman who was escorted into the courtroom this morning was totally different. Mr. Schaberg, her lawyer, had done a good job getting Launie ready for the trial. She was dressed in a plain blue skirt and a frilly blouse which still struggled to cover her huge breasts but it wasn't vulgar by any means. Her face had very little make-up on it and my eyes were drawn to several scars on her face that appeared to be caused by being burned. Her cheeks were more pronounced now that she had lost so much weight.

She caught me staring at her and turned to look at me with eyes that were clear and had emotion in them. I saw her hands and the long fake nails which were stained with tobacco that I remember from that time at the High Tide were gone and her own nails were short and had what looked like clear polish on them. She really looked like a conservative middle age housewife.

We had all heard about her hitting the guard and waddling frantically down the hall of the third floor of the jail thinking she would go through the big window at the end and land in the Sound but instead had landed on the hard dirt below. We kept track of her stay in the hospital with broken ribs, broken nose, and concussions. Her stay there had undoubtedly postponed the trial—postponed it for the first time.

One of our biggest laughs as we ate together at one of our Socials was Bicycle Bob's version of Launie running. He entered the banquet room from the kitchen huffing and puffing and waddling from side to side as he headed straight for one of the windows that overlook our small pool. He had come to a screeching halt and turned and laughed the 'Bob" laugh.

The same guard Launie had overpowered, a short woman probably close to thirty years old, was with J C Blevins as they walked Launie into the courtroom and now stood behind her as she sat at the defense table.

I remembered that poster which was plastered about town when Launie first opened her place. It showed her standing in a provocative pose beckoning you to come visit her. Part of that attractiveness had returned now—the hideous clown was gone.

I realized it was her eyes that I remember from that poster. Now they were sharp, attacking, and continually searching the faces of the jury. I got the feeling she was looking for a particular person, but that may just be my imagination.

I would kick myself for the rest of the trial because when I look at Launie I hear lines from that song from back in the 1980's about Bette Davis eyes. She had once been a truly remarkable and uniquely attractive woman staring with those eyes, but Launie's stare even now could transfix you.

"She'll unease you" and "she'll lay you on her throne" and "she'll make a pro blush" and "she'll throw you like a dice" with her "precocious" eyes...

4

Here Comes Trouble

I sit on my balcony most afternoons after three o'clock with exactly three ounces of wine in my big red plastic tumbler that advertises Fort Walton Beach and which probably holds at least a pint. I measure it carefully and savor it as I sit and watch the visitors, the people who work here, and my neighbors and I learn a lot. Visitors leave usually on Sunday mornings and by that evening, La Mancha is full of new vacationers who come to our beautiful beach. As I remember the hundreds of students I had in class over the years and how each of them was unique, the same is true for our visitors. I guess I just like to watch people.

As I sit on my usual tall bar stool, I think how Bicycle Bob always teases me about drinking exactly three ounces of wine, but I remind him that Brother Paul in the Good Book tells me that wine is good for my stomach. Besides, six or eight White Russians like Bob puts away every twenty-four hours has got to be having a bum effect on his liver. He has a plastic mug that has a lid with a hole for a straw and I think he has cut a straw down to fit the height of the mug for it is just above the rim. About the only time you don't see him with the mug full of White Russians is when he's riding his bicycle. Last week Gladis Kinnaird suggested in her serious way that he ought to fix a strap on the mug so go around his neck so he can sip as he goes.

Judge Bickel had announced yesterday that there would be no court session today as he had some personal business to attend to. I was happy about having nothing to do as I sat in the late afternoon sun, but then I saw one of those sudden summer storms forming on the western horizon of the barren sands of the Eglin Air Command.

Suddenly the weather horns at Navarre, about ten miles to the west started blaring their distinctive blast. A few seconds later the horns at Mary Ester joined in only to be followed quickly by the ones at Fort Walton Beach. The really big horns at Eglin Air Base joined in and in a couple of minutes the ones at Destin followed. We obviously had some bad weather headed toward us.

The La Mancha is the last condo complex on Santa Rosa Blvd and bumps up against a really ugly unkempt chain link fence that is about twenty feet high; on the other side are barren sand mounds which were stripped of their pine groves by Ivan several years ago. Scrub bushes and new pines are trying to regain footholds with sporadic bunches of sea oats and bitter switch grass struggling just as hard to hold the sand in place--but mainly the area is barren for at least five miles to our west.

I see the fast moving ominous black clouds hurrying toward us and could see the line where the heavy rain was moving with them. Thunder blasted through the air and echoed off the Gulf and Sound. The sky was a spider web of lightning which snapped and sputtered in one place to suddenly jump to another place. Spider webs filled my view and I grew apprehensive as I sat there out in the open on my balcony, but something stopped me from leaving.

Suddenly a water spout appeared out from the shore in the Gulf; it was growing larger and larger as it sped toward the shore. People from the Midwest know what tornados are and that is just what a water spout is—a swirling mass of extremely fast wind that's filled with water and debris it picks up as it goes along.

I see Henry Embser, our new beach attendant, run across the sand warning people to get off the beach and start lowering umbrellas and throwing them flat on the sand. He grabbed a chair, collapsed it flat, threw it on some umbrellas to hold them down, I guess, and hurried to get another one. There were too many umbrellas and too many of those heavy lounge chairs, I thought.

As I had been looking at him, I turned back toward the spout and see that it is much closer and much, much larger now and was completely over the sand of the Air Command. Getting bigger and bigger around, it looked to me to be way over two hundred feet into the air. I am filled with wonder as I comprehend that it is strong enough to pull thousands of gallons of water that high in the air.

When Ivan went through the Island all the growth—the pine grove of trees thirty to forty feet tall, the half dozen Live Oak trees which had survived previous hurricanes, the undergrowth of azaleas, saw palmetto, and wiregrass—was ripped from the ground and went tumbling across the Sound into Fort Walton Beach. New growth sprang miraculously from the barren sand and was making a strong come back, but I now I see the little pines and shrubs ripped up into the spout.

It swirled and wobbled from side-to-side like a drunken sailor and finally crossed over the Island and went whirling into the water of the Sound. I have no idea what the effect of that water had on the spout but it erratically jumped back on the barren sand and zigzagging back and forth, cut a wide swath as it headed straight for the La Mancha.

Henry saw it and ran as fast as he could in the heavy downpour which the spout had pushed in on us, toward the new reconstructed gazebo that sits close to the beach immediately in front of the big Y shaped pool. I must have looked like a fool as I found myself jumping and shouting for Henry and all the beach goers to run faster.

Out of the corner of my eye I see Daniel Sheraton, Henry's boss and manager of all the beach attendants on the Island, pull up in his Ford F150. Daniel is about thirty two-or-three but built like all the guys he hires, strong and fast. He dashed down the sidewalk by the pool, down the boardwalk and on down the ramp from the gazebo and shouted for Henry to help him. They were frantically dragging chairs and umbrellas up close to the gazebo, but like I already knew, there were too many of them.

As the water spout hit our beach it was full of sand, along with drift wood and I saw a bright beach towel whirling around and around within it until it was flipped out of the top way above our heads. It really looked extremely dangerous up this close to us so I got down on the floor of my balcony and watch it approach through the ornate railing. It smashed into the low crenulated stout rock wall that surrounds the perimeter of the La Mancha as the whirling saw-like ring of sand was ripping through the little fences strung along the beach to keep the sand from blowing away. As the whirring ring bounced along the rock wall, I heard a gnawing like a power saw ripping through a two-by-four.

I watch in amazement as Daniel and Henry run away from it and go hurdling over the railing into the ditch where the beach sunflowers and sea oats flourish from the shower water where the beach goers wash the sand off when they come up from the beach. I watch in some kind of weird fascination as the spout starts tearing off planks from the west steps to the beach and from the west boardwalk.

Hitting the perimeter wall had caused the spout to roll erratically again and for what seemed two or three minutes it sat still in one place spinning out a deep hole in our beach and spitting out whirling rings of sand. Then, just as quickly as it started, it jerked to the right and spewed out over the Gulf.

Beach chairs and umbrellas whirl around and around into the center of the spout as they were caught up in it as it left the beach. Suddenly one umbrella snapped open and spun to the top of the spout where it looked like one of those little paper umbrellas stuck into a drink. It rotated slower and slower and looked like a spinning top on the floor as it slows down ready to fall. It was spit out of the top and went sailing way off into the water.

The spout was full of many fish and lots of seaweed along with gallons and gallons of water. I looked in amazement as a small sand shark fell out of the swirl and went flopping down followed by what looked like many, many Red Fish.

Jonathan L and his many relatives trailed far behind the spout and circled and dove down at the free lunch which had fallen out. One of the shrieking relatives got too close to the spout and was sucked in. I saw that gull swirl around and around as it was thrown to the top just like the umbrella had been and then spit out to fall toward the water. I knew it was dead because it fell like a rock.

It didn't take more than five minutes from when I had first seen the spout form until it disappeared toward the horizon.

Daniel was the first one to appear in my sight as he crawled out from under what now was a mass of sticks and brush. Then I saw Henry struggle out of another spot. I guess I must have been hollering a lot louder than I thought for they turned and waved in my direction giving me a thumbs up.

Umbrellas and chairs were scattered all around and probably thirty or so were smashing about in the angry waves, some way out in the Gulf. The rain was coming down harder than ever as Daniel and Henry rushed up to get inside the gazebo.

As I picked up my chair which I had overturned and stood back from the railing so I wouldn't get soaked, I saw a strange object out on the sand not far from the shore of the Gulf, but in the Command where the spout had cut a wide swath. I couldn't believe what I saw so I got my binoculars that hang on a hook on the wall of the balcony and discovered I wasn't imagining things.

Sitting out in the open sand where the spout had ripped out the path was a large sandy and orange colored cat dripping wet but standing boldly out in the open. I suppose I should say a huge sandy and orange cat for I don't think I have ever seen a bigger one, but where in the world could it have come from? It sat there—sitting straight up and very tall-- soaking wet but with its ears perked up and staring straight at us. Even though its fur was matted down against it sides, I could see the big paws and the strong muscles of its legs and sides.

I didn't know it then but this would not be the last adventure that Daniel and Henry and the cat would have, and the next one would be deadly.

5
Poseidon

As the storm was disappearing quickly out over the Gulf and the rain had nearly stopped my cell phone rang, I pulled it out of my pocket and saw that it was from Gladis, my friend who lives in her beautiful condo on the bottom floor of the Dolphin which is the building straight across from me on the other side of the big pool.

My first reaction was for her safety, "Are you okay?" I shouted.

"You don't have to holler now. Can't you see me standing on my porch?"

She stood waving and I sheepishly waved back, "Is there any damage over there, I ask?"

"Just to my nerves," she laughed. "I was standing looking out the window to the west when I saw it forming so I ran into my bathroom and stayed until I got too curious and came back out to see what was happening."

"I was pretty scared too, but I watched the whole thing except when I couldn't see what was happening on the other side of your building."

Then I thought of the cat. "Turn around and look at what is sitting out there in the sand."

As she turned, I saw her gasp with surprise and she quickly went inside her sliding patio doors, "What the hell is that?" She was the one shouting now.

"I have no idea where it came from, but I'm sure glad you see it too because I would get laughed out of the place if I am the only one that can see it. Wait a minute, I want Daniel and Henry to see it too."

I shouted as loud as I could down to them and pointed past the warning sign that indicates the beginning of the Air Command. They turned to look and I saw their reaction; they were just as startled as Gladis and me.

Daniel came down the boardwalk and stood on the sidewalk right underneath my balcony, "Where in God's world did that come from?"

"I don't know," I hollered. "I was watching you and Henry trying to save the beach stuff and turned around and there it sat."

"You think it was caught up in the spout?"

"I don't know, but I have never seen it before."

"That is the biggest cat I have ever seen. That must be at least thirty pounds. What do we do with it now?"

Reverend Crabtree had appeared around the corner of the Pelican and was standing on the concert pad where the sidewalks intersect, "It is from the Evil One... Sent to bring Judgement on all of you... Harken to my Warning for I know the Truth."

Daniel and Henry who I guess had never seen our resident Prophet stared and then backed away from him.

Bicycle Bob came wheeling around the corner of the Dolphin, saw Gladis who was now back out on her porch, came to a sudden stopped and I heard him say, "You, okay, Gladis?" This was Bob. I was just surprised it took him so long to get over here from Sea Shell building but then I thought about how hard the rain had been and he had waited till it had slacked up, I guess.

Gladis pointed out past the west boardwalk and said, "Look out there."

"Holly shit! Oops, excuse, me Gladis. Damn it to hell where did that come from?"

By now, there were several people either out on their balconies or walking around on the lawn or headed toward the gazebo. I hurried out my door, got on the elevator and anxiously waited for the trip down the three floors—our elevators are slow.

By the time I got out to where Daniel, Henry, Bob and Gladis were now standing by the wall that surrounds the property, everyone out there had seen the cat.

Reverend Crabtree started his spiel again, "Beware all you who are heathens…"

Bob cut him off, "Sir, you are a damn moron who will harm us all before that stinking cat will. Get away from here. Now!"

Crabtree thrust his staff onto the concrete rapidly three or four times, and left.

A precocious little girl of three or four pointed her finger at the cat and said, "Look, daddy, it's from the water. Its name is Poseidon." Her daddy laughed and said, "Yes, Kiera, it came from somewhere for sure, so it might as well be Poseidon."

And that name stuck. During the rest of the summer Poseidon caused a lot of concern and a lot of entertainment around the La Mancha, but it was in late October when he became so important to us.

6

Letting a Rookie do the Job

Judge Bickel came through his door.

The bailiff told us all to rise.

Bickel is a tall thin man who appears to go to the gym regularly. He's considered very handsome from what I hear from the women around town. Behind the bench which is raised above the courtroom floor he really is the dominant figure in the room.

"Before we get started with today's proceedings, let me remind everyone involved (he turned to look at both the Prosecution and Defense tables), this is a trial about how the man who has become known as 'Ollie' died. The trial is about absolutely nothing else, and I will stop the trial if all parties do not follow these instructions. If anyone in the courtroom has questions about what I am saying, let it be known now."

Judge Bickel looked at both the Defense table and the Prosecutor's table again and said, "Mr. Porter, you may start today's proceedings by calling your witness."

"Thank you, Your Honor, the prosecution calls Katrina Hart to the stand."

There was a buzz around the room, and Bicycle Bob nudged my foot. I turned and glared at him as the young woman who was helping J C Blevins bring Launie Sanderson to and from the courtroom walked up to the witness stand. I had never seen her before and I was curious how she had gained the confidence of the court after the episode she had with Launie at the jail.

After she was sworn in, Porter cleared his throat which brought a grunt from Bob for we had laughed last night that when Porter clears his throat the witness better watch out.

"Miss Hart, what do you do for a living?"

"I work for the County as a guard at the jail."

"Were you on duty when Launie Sanderson's lawyer came to see her?"

"Yes sir, I stood outside the door as Mr. Schaberg was in the room talking to her."

"Now, is there a window in that door?"

Curtis Porter has been the County Prosecutor for at least ten years. His family had moved to Okaloosa County many years ago from Holton, Kansas and his grandfather had served the County as Presiding Judge for over twenty-five years before his death in 2001. Curt resembled his grandfather in many ways; he is well over six feet tall, has a strong square chin and piercing blue eyes.

Perhaps his offensive habit if he has one, is that he stops in the middle of a question or sentence and loudly clears this throat as Bob and I had laughed about. After a while, we realized it was his way of pausing just before he struck out at a witness or made a very important point.

"Yes, almost the whole top half is heavy glass that's reinforced with a wire mesh between the layers of glass."

"Did you see Launie Sanderson's lawyer give her anything?"

Schaberg was on his feet shouting, "Objection, Your Honor. The Defense lawyer is certainly allowed to share papers and evidence with his client."

"Sustained. Mr. Porter, you know better."

"Yes, Your Honor, I do." He paused and carefully cleared his throat, "Now, Miss Hart, did you see Mr. Schaberg give Launie Sanderson anything besides papers?"

"Your Honor, he certainly didn't listen to you..."

"Mr. Porter, you better know what you are doing asking this question again after I told you not to. Be prepared to pay for this..."

"Miss Hart, I believe you need to answer my question," Porter said.

"I ah, I saw him take his handkerchief out of his coat pocket and hand it to her. She was screaming and crying for some reason. That's when I opened the door and said the meeting was over."

"Did she give the handkerchief back to him?"

"I don't remember. She must have because she didn't have it later."

"Miss Hart, how long had you worked for the Sheriff's office at that time?"

"Just a few weeks."

"Don't you think it was strange that you would be the one to escort Launie Sanderson, a prisoner accused of first degree murder to and from her cell?"

Schaberg looked like he was going to have a seizure, but Porter said, "I remove that question" before Schaberg could speak.

Judge Bickel had his gavel raised into the air ready to slam it on the block of hard wood on his desk, but Porter went on as Bickel glared at him.

"Miss Hart, has anyone in the police station questioned you or talked about why you should have not have been fired for what happened next that day?"

"Your Honor, I demand that this stop. Mr. Porter is putting words into her mouth and accusing her of being an accessory to something or other," Schaberg roared as he was half way to Bickel's bench.

"Withdraw the question. Now, Miss Hart, it's true that Launie Sanderson overpowered you and ran down the halls of the jail and finally crashed through a window at the end of one of them?"

"Yes."

"Did you hear her say or holler anything as she was running down the hallway?"

She looked again at the Defense table like she was asking Schaberg to object but when he didn't she replied, "Yes, she was hollering and screaming as she ran down the hall."

"And did you hear what she was hollering and screaming?"

"Well, I can't be sure…"

"Miss Hart, you are under oath to tell the truth…"

She looked again at Schaberg but he seemed like he wasn't about to get involved in this, "She was hollering that she was dying… that she was poisoned… that the pain would be too great…that she rather drown than have that pain."

"She said what?"

"She was screaming that she wouldn't be able to stand the pain."

"What do you think she meant?" Err... ah... withdraw the question, Your Honor. "As she was running, was she doing anything unusual?"

"Well, she was extremely heavy, obese actually, and she was panting and heaving. She was holding her stomach too."

"Holding her stomach? Like it hurt?"

"I really can't answer that, Mr. Porter, because you know I have no experience and am not a doctor."

The courtroom burst into laughter and Judge Bickel slammed down his gavel.

Porter cleared his throat and rubbed his chin. I felt a sharp kick to my leg.

Okay, Miss Hart, "Did you notice anything unusual about the way she had been acting the last two weeks since she had been a prisoner?"

"I don't know what you mean...."

"Were you there when Launie Sanderson was first arrested and put into a cell?"

"Yes, I had been there for a few weeks."

"When she first came in, was she acting strangely?"

"Objection, Your Honor. How would Miss Hart know how Launie Sanderson had acted before?"

"Sustain. Mr. Porter restate you question or go on to something else."

"Miss Hart, were you the one assigned to Launie Sanderson when she was first brought to the jail?"

"Yes, I gave her medicines and was stationed outside her door."

"Why? Did Launie Sanderson needed medicine? What medicine?"

Katrina Hart looked in the direction of the Defense table where Launie was looking at her with a look I had never seen before. Her eyes were filled with hate.

"She acted like she was on some kind of stimulant or something when she first came. She would scream that she needed 'her fix' over and over again."

Schaberg was fit to be tied, "Your Honor the Defense requests that the witness' last statement be stricken from the record and that the jury be instructed to ignore it."

"Mr. Schaberg, I don't see any reason to sustain your complaint. Mr. Porter asked Miss Hart why she was stationed outside Miss Sanderson's cell and what medicines she was to give Miss Sanderson.

"Your Honor, the Prosecution is finished with this witness."

"Court will recess until ten in the morning." Judge Bickel announce and hurriedly got up and disappeared through the door behind him.

The people in the room were suddenly quiet and many were staring at each other, the jury looked like it couldn't believe that court was recessing this early in the afternoon, and Bob said, "Something a little fishy is going on, me thinks!"

Gladis, Bob, and I sat on Bob's balcony in the Sea Shell building that night enjoying one of his famous grilled sirloins and many—too many—drinks. His balcony overlooks the dark water of the Sound and tonight a most unusually beautiful sunset was reflected on the still water below.

27

Gladis had remarked that she didn't think very much got done today. Bob agreed, but I said, "I think Porter was just showing how much he might know about what was happening that day when Schaberg visited Launie the first time."

It was getting late as I walked Gladis back to her building and went on around the corner and headed over to my building.

Standing in the gazebo was one of Reverend Crabtree's entourage, the one they call Eva I hear. She was talking with someone that I could not see back in the shadows.

7

Tripped

The next morning Judge Bickel entered the courtroom at precisely ten o'clock, sat down at his desk and announced. "Mr. Schaberg, yesterday we recessed court as Mr. Porter said he was finished questioning Katrina Hart. Do you have questions for this witness?"

"Your Honor, the Defense would like the prerogative to call Miss Hart at a later time?'

"Granted. Mr. Porter, you may call your next witness."

"The Prosecution calls Dr. Kevin Wells."

After the coroner was sworn in, Porter said, "Dr. Wells, how long have you been the Coroner for Okaloosa County?"

Dr. Wells is one of those pleasant faced people who just seem to get easier to live with as they get older. He must be at least seventy years old, but looks like he's fifty something.

"Since 2002."

"As Coroner, are you the Chief Medical Officer for Okaloosa County?"

"That's right."

"What did you do before you became Coroner?"

"I was in private practice for some years as a GP."

"You mean General Practitioner?"

"That's right."

"You said, for some years?"

"Almost forty."

Porter smiled and smiled bigger as he turned to the jury, "Dr. Wells, you must have been a teenager when you started practicing medicine. Would you mind telling us how 'young' you are?"

The Doctor smiled and replied, "I was 76 on July 19."

"You could have fooled me and I'd wager a lot of other people in this room. Now, how many autopsies have you perform?"

"Three last year and one this year."

"No, sir, I mean altogether."

"Goodness, Mr. Porter, I wouldn't know off-hand. Several though."

"Who were the ones last year, Doctor?"

"That young woman found on the beach in front of the La Mancha who had her arms cut off just below the elbow though they were hacked several times and therefore were jaggedly cut, that other woman who washed up on the same beach who had died of a blunt force to her head, and the man we are all calling, 'Ollie.'"

Schaberg was red with anger, "Your Honor, I move to strike the references to the two women as they have nothing to do with this trial."

"Sustained. Mr. Porter, you are doing it again. I remind you this trial is about the killing of the man we call 'Ollie' and nothing else."

"Yes, Your Honor. Now, Dr. Wells, can you tell us how 'Ollie' died?"

"Yes, he was shot in the back of the head where his head connected to the top of his spinal cord by a small caliber gun. He was shot one time. He was probably dead before he slumped over and smeared his own blood on that plastic cover that was on that comic book."

Schaberg was furious, "Your Honor, the Coroner isn't answering the question. He's telling a story."

"Sustained."

"Okay, Dr. Wells, can you give us an educated estimation as to the time Ollie was killed?"

"The police report says that Launie Sanderson was apprehended in front of that little dock over where her business once stood at 11:15 p.m. The eye witnesses to the shooting say that they looked at a cell phone used to call 911 and report the shooting at 10:23 p.m."

Schaberg was on his feet again, "Your Honor, Dr. Wells is once again telling a story and the Defense objects."

"Overruled as the Court finds he is setting up how he determined the time of death. Proceed, Dr. Wells."

Doctor Wells glanced at Porter and there was a hint of a smile, "But my real evidence as to the time is because the police were able to get the body out of the water quickly because they knew where to go to find it. When I arrived I found the body was still 'warm' when I got there shortly after midnight, so I'm saying Ollie was killed between 10 p.m. and midnight on that October night."

"I'm sorry to ask this question with a certain person in the room, but Dr. Wells you said the body was still 'warm.' What do you mean by that term?"

I saw Schaberg turn and lean in to talk with Launie Sanderson when Porter said the remark about a certain person in the room. Launie shrugged her shoulders and they both turned to listen to what was being said.

"The blood had not settled and rigor mortis had not begun at all and that water was cold."

Porter cleared his throat and ran his hand across his board square chin, "Now, Dr. Wells, did you examine Laune Sanderson when you returned to Fort Walton Beach after examining Ollie's body out there on the Sound close to Mary Ester?"

"Yes."

"What did you find?"

"I found clear evidence that she had GSR under the nails of her right hand even though I was told by the police that she had been to the restroom and had washed her hands again and again."

"For those of us who might not know what GSR is, will you please define that for us?"

"I'm sorry. With so many crime shows on television, I thought that GSR, or gunshot residue, was familiar to most people."

"Dr. Wells, how did you know that GSR was under her nails for certain?"

"I made a melted paraffin wax cast of her right hand—the hand she herself said was her dominant hand—and used diphenylamine and sulfuric acid in the cast. Blue specks were all over the inside of the cast which indicated that nitrates from the gun powder were present."

"Thank you Dr. Wells. That's all the questions I have for the Coroner, Your Honor."

"Your witness, Mr. Schaberg."

Schaberg walked slowly toward the witness chair. When he arrived there, he turned his back to Dr. Wells and looked straight at the jury.

"Dr. Well, have you ever cheated when you have done an autopsy?"

"No, sir. Not intentionally."

Schaberg made a dramatic whirl to face the doctor, "Are you going to say that you didn't withhold details of the second woman's body that was found on the beach last summer? That you failed to report some facts from you autopsy report?"

Porter was definitely smiling as he stood and objected, "Your Honor, not fifteen minutes ago Mr. Schaberg himself reminded me and this court that this trial has nothing to do with the bodies of those two women. So, naturally I object and request that his question be stricken from the record."

"Sustained. Mr. Schaberg, it appears you have made a serious mistake. Anything else you wish to ask the coroner?"

"No, Your Honor," Schaberg replied, as he quickly walked back to the Defense table.

Launie Sanderson looked like she could kill him on the spot.

8
Reginald Graham Robert Bakersfield

We have many aircraft that fly over our section of the Island every day, Raptors with their strange wing propellers, a big old C130 that rookie pilots from Eglin train in and that worries me many times a week for it flies so low and makes sharp and quick turns right over the La Mancha, helicopters that fly back and forth from Eglin to Panama City almost every day as they skirt the shore very close to the beach, and those little private planes that pull the banners which advertise businesses for the tourists to see like, *High Tide the Best Seafood,* or *Helen Back Pizza,* and my favorite *Alvins Island 70% Off* (Alvins Island is always 70% off).

My friend, Ryan Tilley, owns one of those little planes but Ryan is now at Gator Land in Gainsville studying to be an ichthyologist and his friend Freddie is flying the plane and pulling the signs.

But the 'aircrafts' I enjoy the most and am amazed about are the Brown pelicans which fly west every morning and east every evening in flocks of thirty to fifty and many trips back and forth during the day in much smaller flocks. I don't know where they are going nor what they are doing and I'm sure they don't do it for me, but they amaze me. I have thought before just how those clumsy clowns who wobbled down a pier--sometimes even falling over--can form into an almost perfect V and with little flapping they glide and sail through the air with superb grace. I guess the older I get, the less it takes me to get emotional about what I think beauty is.

There must be an air current which helps propel them along as they swoop in very close to our two buildings and out again as they pass the La Mancha. Sometimes they get so close to the Pelican building that I can see the real prehistoric features of their heads; they remind me of pterodactyls. But their grace and apparent concern for each other erases from my mind anything sinister about them.

I'm sitting here on my balcony this morning with my hot coffee with so much half-in-half in it that it looks more like chocolate milk than coffee as I see Jonathan L. swoop in and land on the volleyball goat post. For yet another silly reason, that makes me feel good.

I named Jonathan L over a year ago as I noticed there was always a gull sitting on the top of the volleyball goal post closest to the Gulf. I know it is probably not the same gull but I decided that I would say it was. He always seemed to be there and to be alone.

I gave a copy of *Jonathan Livingstone Seagull* by Richard Bach to Paul Bishop who I was tutoring then. Paul became very important to me and use to sit on the stone wall right in front of where the volleyball goal is further out on the sand. He sat there alone and together he and that bird became 'friends.'

Later when Paul was killed in the shocking accident on Highway 98 we had his funeral on the beach and when his best friend pushed his long board with his ashes on it out into the water Jonathan L. suddenly flew straight up into the sky and soared overhead.

Yes, I know, I'm an old man who finds the symbolic elements in that, but it did happen. Now, I go down and sit in the same place on the rock wall often and see Jonathan L out on his perch and see the single stalk of sea oats I planted up against the wall there. Remarkably it is straight and taller than the other sea oats that were planted along the wall to hold the sand in place. It reminds me of Paul as he use to get on his long board and paddle out into the water—straight and tall—a new Huck Finn on his raft on his water.

The bicycle comes zooming around the corner of Dolphin building across from me and Bob starts squeezing the Groucho Marks horn with glee. His eyes are almost slits as his big smile covers his face. He sees me sitting on the wall and shouts a loud "Morning" to me and goes almost skidding into the gazebo. He pauses and looks out at the beach and the Gulf, makes a U turn and pumps vigorously up the boardwalk, whizzes close by me as he barrels down the sidewalk and turns to zip around the end of my building. I hear the horn going 'ooga ooga' as he disappears.

My friend Bob, master of the laugh, hardheaded as a granite mountain, and protector of the La Mancha, starts the party when he arrives. My thoughts turn to what Bob has told me of himself and what I have learned from his friends and acquaintances.

Surprisingly he confided in me what his real name is, "Reginald Graham Robert Bakersfield is what they tied on me. I grew up without a care in the world till I started school. My dad was really respected around Fort Walton Beach and there was always plenty of money for just about anything I wanted. He was Catholic but my mom wasn't but that never caused me any problems. I realized at an early age that I couldn't measure up to what Dad wanted of me. We lived in a big sprawling house overlooking the Bay over on Brooks Street—named after the same Mayor as the bridge is."

The enormous Choctawhatchee Bay begins right after the Santa Rosa Sound goes under Brooks Bridge which connects the mainland with Okaloosa Island. Bob had told me one night as we sat on his balcony over at Sea Shell building drinking—me a margarita and him the usual White Russians-- that he tried to walk all the way across the bay one night when he was around twenty, drunk, and had made a bet with one of his buddies. He burst out in his loud raucous laugh as he finished telling me that someone had to pull him out of the water into a boat to save him.

He said, "That black water of the Sound out there," he pointed to the glistening flat water just about two hundred yards in front of his balcony, "starts over at Pensacola and runs about thirty-five miles until it empties into the Bay. It's dark, almost black water. That's where Okaloosa County gets its name as 'Okaloosa' is the Choctaw Indian word for 'Blackwater.' The Sound is usually as wide as a good size river but sometimes narrows into maybe only a couple of hundred yards wide—that's how it is right here at Fort Walton Beach."

He was called Reggie in the first grade until a little girl starting reciting his name as she jumped rope and the other boys teased him about having a 'girlfriend.' He spent one afternoon in Sister Mary Martha's outer office for pulling that little girl's hair as he got in her face to not ever do that again. He sat all afternoon because his parents were out on one of their boats and didn't know he was in trouble at the little Catholic school. He said, "My Dad wouldn't have cared anyway for he seldom knew what I was doing at school."

The rest of elementary school he was called Graham because he hated Reginald and thought Graham sounded 'grand' and also Southern.

But when he went to Choctaw High School, he became Bobbie one night when a sophomore girl whispered it in his ear as they parked down at the Nature Center. He was just a freshman but was already known around school because he was the only freshman on the varsity football team. That's what he called himself all through high school and for many years later because he would never have let his buddies know his whole name.

He shuffled his way through Choctaw High School and was interested in three things: football, the opposite sex, and marijuana. He succeeded with all three as he became what many called 'the best running back in Florida,' made his many trips down to the Nature Center at night with an adoring and usually a very pretty and cooperative coed, and shared his money to buy and share with his friends the best marijuana. During the four years he was the starting wide receiver for the Big Green Indians, his dad never saw him play.

After finishing high school, he had no desire to go to any of the colleges who came to Fort Walton Beach to talk with him. Instead, with long straight hair that fell over his shoulders, a hot car, and plenty of stash to roll a dozen joints, he started carousing about the area racing speed boats and catamarans and chasing any new women he discovered. His dad started the Yacht Club and Bobby had all the benefits of using several high-powered and luxurious boats.

At one time, he had so many trophies on his shelves from winning every one of the annual races from Panama City to Pensacola and some from over in Mobile Bay that he didn't have any more room.

Then he became bored with the racing and settled in on two things, chasing women and drinking. Many of his friends often talked about how it's a wonder he's alive to tell the many tales he enjoys so much. That turned out to be an accurate prediction for one drunken trip down Highway 85 from up north, he slammed his almost new Camaro into the railing at the bridge at Shalimar and went flying into the Cinco Bayou.

He almost killed himself; it took the rescue team several hours to get him out of the wreck which was in twenty to thirty feet of water. Miraculously an air bubble inside the car had saved him. They rushed him to the helicopter pad at Sacred Heart but didn't even unload him as the doctor in charge told them to get him to Pensacola. After hours of surgery and being pronounced dead twice, he finally pulled through and after spending several in the hospital, his folks moved him into their condo at the La Mancha.

When both his parents had passed away, Bob was left with the condo at the La Mancha, a little dock over on Lake Earl, an inlet off the Choctawhatchee Bay, and his fishing boat, *The Choctaw Pride*. He hasn't lost his joy of fishing almost every weekend and almost always he takes his boat out into the Gulf, fishes all day Saturday, sleeps on the boat, and returns to the dock late Sunday afternoon after fishing till noon. Several months ago, he began fishing every Wednesday too which seemed a little strange to me, but as he said, "What else do I have to do?"

I have enjoyed many a meal of fresh caught fish either on his balcony or from my own grill that he has brought back to the La Mancha.

When I came to the La Mancha, Bob was one of the first to make me feel at home. By this time, he sure had changed physically. Because of the horrible car wreck, he had to slow down and he really did. Now, Bicycle Bob is a pretty hefty bald fifty-something who hangs over his bicycle seat on all sides when he makes his usual three trips around the property every day and then retires to sit about one of the pools or on some balcony to drink White Russians.

I thought he would be turned-off when he found out I was a retired teacher who moved here from Albuquerque to find my home in a condo overlooking the waters of the Gulf, but Bob just laugh with that animated laugh of his and dubbed me "Prof."

Not too much happens around the La Mancha complex that Bob doesn't know or help make decisions about. He is the Chairman of the Condo Owners Association and knows more about the six big Spanish looking buildings which make up the complex than anyone else except maybe Bette who is the manager of the place.

Bob could and does finagle his way into and out of many things, and I may have said it before but I wondered how he gets a pass to be in Judge Bickel's court every day.

9

Ester Haynes

J C Blevins stood ten feet behind the Defense table, just far enough that if someone lunged at him he would have time to evade them. He felt his state issued revolver on his belt and looked over at Katrina Hart who was at the metal detector at the entrance to the courtroom. He and Miss Hart were the only two people allowed to have firearms in the courtroom. He was not too sure that Miss Hart could handle herself with a gun after what he had heard yesterday in the courtroom.

The two lawyers were at Judge Bickel's bench discussing something in low voices that he could not hear. He was getting tired of this trail, just like the Prof had told him he was. He liked the Prof who he had met last summer when all that trouble broke loose out at the La Mancha.

He wondered why he stuck with this job with its dangers and long hours. It sure wasn't because of the money—about the only lower paid professional were those poor dedicated teachers who put up with today's teenagers.

J C grew up in Destin which is the biggest tourist destination in the area and had been on the force for seven years when the first body washed up in front of the La Mancha. Until that time, he spent most days parking beside busy Highway 98 so he could slow down or stop speeders. He was only responsible for Okaloosa County as three or four million tourist come into the County each year to vacation with their families on the beautiful white sands next to the emerald Gulf or come in the winter months to escape the cold from up in New England and even Canada. He had become a trooper just out of the two years of college he spent at North West Florida up at Niceville.

40

Blevins is a tall stout young man about thirty five years old with an easy smile and happy disposition. During the investigation of the first body and later of the body of Josephine Jones, he had kept the Okaloosa County Detective on a steady course with his likable personality. The detective had been impatient and abrupt with people while Blevins was quiet and made people comfortable.

Then, when Ollie was killed in the middle of the Sound which is State Property, Blevins suddenly found himself in charge of the investigation. Sometimes he regretted the responsibility of being in charge of this horrific case which had gained so much publicity. He knew things about Launie Sanderson that had nothing to do with the murder of Ollie, but which Judge Bickel was determined to keep out of this trial.

He was smart enough to patrol around and then sit quietly in his patrol car secluded from sight near Launie's place and he had recorded many license plates which were regular customers even though they were from other states.

He had put the cuffs on Launie that night he and others had raced through Fort Walton Beach on a tip from that young couple who saw the murder as she walked up the gravel path from the little dock where she had tied-up that huge yacht of hers. Early the next morning he saw two cabs pull up and the drivers started loading many pieces of luggage, so much that some of it had to be tied to the racks on the tops. He saw both cabs fill up with Launie's girls and as he followed them they turned onto Memorial Drive until they reached the entrance to Memorial Cemetery where they turned in. He pulled in behind them and went across the way quite a distance where he took as many pictures as he could with the long lens of his camera. He was afraid they would notice him but they were too engrossed in what they were doing.

He saw them surround the fresh covered grave and one-by-one lay something by the new tombstone. Helping one of them in particular,

41

they got back into the cabs and headed for the Destin-Fort Walton Beach Airport at Valparaiso.

He followed and parked his car and went into the airport after waiting long enough, he thought, for them to get their tickets and go to their departure gate. He was just in time to hear an agent at the United Counter exclaim to another agent, "Did you see that? They all paid their tickets to Memphis with $50 bills. I have a whole drawer full of $50 bills!"

Blevins had learned all he needed to know.

Even though they had the eye-witnesses to the murder, District Attorney Curtis Porter wanted more evidence about what had happened at Launie's place the days before the murder. Blevins and Porter talked for hours about what to do, and it was decided that he would go to Memphis to try and locate one or more of the women.

Memphis is the biggest metropolitan area on the Mississippi River and is sprawled out on hundreds of acres as the land around the city is very flat. Blevins slogged through the mud of West Memphis, Arkansas more times than he could remember. He heard the Blues so much he developed a keen hatred for it. He spent over three months 'living' on Beale Street at nights and traveling many of the shabby streets where there were 'houses' on every block and working girls on every corner, but he had no luck and he returned to Fort Walton Beach to an unhappy Porter.

A few weeks afterwards he was driving down Memorial Drive and as he passed the cemetery he remembered the women had laid something around the tombstone and he was curious. He slowly drove his trooper's car into the drive and stopped a few yards from where he thought the grave was. He got out and started walking to it and then saw one of the young women sitting on a bench over at the side of one of the paths. He recognized her immediately for they were all clear in his mind from looking for them and showing their pictures so many times.

42

She saw him and jumped up to leave but as she hurriedly pushed the baby stroller away, he was close behind her, "Wait! I don't mean to arrest you or anything because I have no idea if you have done something wrong."

She stopped and turned to him as he saw she was carrying a grocery sack full of something. "I didn't mean to stay so long," she said.

He saw that her face was stained with tears. "How long have you been back in town?"

"How do you know who I am?" she said quietly.

"I watched when you and the others were here that day when you were going to the airport. I watched all of you put something around his tombstone."

She pushed the stroller back to the bench and sat down and he saw she was weeping uncontrollably now. "Here is what we put on his grave," she said as she dumped the flatten beer cans on the ground. They were not just flatten but crush from end-to-end in little flat medallions. "He did all of these. They use to hang at Launie's place. I just wanted them. I have left them there at his grave for weeks since I came back, but I want them now for his son."

"Miss, my name is J C Blevins. I am working on trying to get Ollie some kind of justice. It's obvious to me that you cared a great deal for him. Will you help me to see that the person who killed him pays for it?"

"Oh, yes. Yes. Mr. Blevins, my name is Ester Haynes. I didn't know what to do and am not brave enough to do away with her by myself but I will help if I can. I was scared to come to the police."

J C sat down beside her, "How long have you been back in Fort Walton Beach and what are you doing to keep you and the baby fed?"

"I was in Memphis about two weeks before he was born," she pull a cover back from the baby's face and ran her hand gently over the top of his head as he was sound asleep. "I couldn't stand being there away from him," she said as she looked over at Ollie's grave, "and I had to bring the baby to show him.... I didn't know anyone here in town but one of the waitresses at the Tides Inn had been nice to me so I called her one night and she met me at the bus station when we got here. She knew this nice lady, Mrs. Kirk, over on Pleasant Street who had a back apartment for rent."

"What do you plan to do?"

"Well, I have to live somewhere and there wasn't anything for me up in Tennessee. I don't have any family that I know about so this was the logical place. I got a job at a grocery store over on Mary Ester Cutoff. It's close enough for me to ride the bus and living on Pleasant Street is close enough for me to push the stroller here to the cemetery."

"How old is the baby?"

"He's old enough to be getting into everything that interests him. He likes to crawl around here on the grass and he likes to play with the medallions. He looks just like his daddy. His name is Mitch."

"Miss Haynes if you help me and Prosecuting Attorney Curtis Porter at Launie Sanderson's trialK it will be a very hard and very long time for you. We are dealing with a ruthless and stubborn defense that will drag you through everything they can think of. But if we have you to tell us first-hand what was going on at her place and what was happening with Ollie, we could very well convict her of Ollie's death as premeditated murder."

"Mr. Blevins, I was one of the girls who worked at her place and did things I am ashamed about. Oh, I didn't do anything unlawful and not anything immoral, but I used my body too convince lots of those men to spend their money at that place. Maybe no one will believe me if I tell what happened there."

"Let's leave that for Mr. Porter to decide. Will you meet with him?"

"Yes… if I can clean-up what I have heard since about how crazy Ollie acted, I must."

"Good. Do you have a phone?"

"Yes, I have to afford a phone because I need to keep in touch with Mrs. Kirk when I'm at work or someplace else. I was really lucky to find her for if she loves him like she loves her grandkids, Mitch is in good hands. I don't think it will be long before he starts calling her Grams like they do. The arrangement has work out so good. She takes care of Mitch during the day and makes some money and I have the opportunity to work."

"Good, I'll call you later this afternoon. In the meantime, watch out for yourself and Mitch. I don't want some people in this town to know you are back. Don't be afraid but don't go to any of the old places that you use to go to."

And now he looked across the courtroom and saw her sitting straight with her arms crossed across her chest like she was trying to be alone and not seen. He must have been staring at her for he realized she was looking back at him. Their eyes met and he smiled at her and thought he saw a timid little smile back.

Suddenly he felt responsible for this woman who he had come to know in the last few months. She is a good mother and from the reports at the grocery store she is a hard worker.

A thought whizzed through his mind that he hadn't considered before; she was very attractive and very interesting. Blevins blushed. He looked around to see if anyone was watching him.

The lawyers had returned to their desks and the clerk was calling the next witness, "Miss Ester Haynes."

10

How we got here

Curt Porter cleared his throat and Bicycle Bob nudged me with the toe of his shoe, "He's on to something."

Judge Jeffery Bickel glared down from his desk high above the courtroom floor and Bob squirmed in his seat. Bob had been told twenty times at least to be quiet in the courtroom, and I was afraid Judge Bickel was going to make him leave.

How Bob gets a pass to be in the courtroom every day is still a mystery to me for many people stood for hours outside the new court house which jutted out over Santa Rosa Sound directly across the Sound from the La Mancha Complex. I had a pass because I had been hired by the *NorthWest Daily* to cover Launie's trial, but Bob had no real reason to be there, but yet he was every day sitting beside me just behind the railing that divided the courtroom.

Bob's whispered comment to me about District Attorney Curtis Porter clearing his throat had become apparent to both of us and we had talked about it as we sat around the big Y shaped pool at the La Mancha. We had realized that when Porter cleared his throat something important was about to happen. That was just one of his habits we had learned during the last several months Launie's trial had been dragging on.

"Now, Miss Haynes, will you tell the court how you came to know Ollie?"

Ester Haynes squirmed in the witness chair much like Bob had done in his chair at few minutes earlier. She was embarrassed and looked afraid of all that was happening around her.

"It's alright, Miss Haynes. Nobody is going to harm you or belittle you for what you are going to say here," Porter clearly and emphatically said as he looked toward the Defense table where Launie Sanderson and her lawyer, Matthew Schaberg, sat staring at her. "Now, go ahead and tell us how you met Ollie."

"It was ten years ago in New Orleans when Katrina almost destroyed the city. I…ah…worked for Launie. The levees had broken with the force of all that water and we had run toward Highway 10. We almost made it, but not quite. We all climbed the fire escape of a building where we thought we would be safe from the wall of water crashing down the streets toward us."

"Who is this 'we' you are talking about? Who was with you?" She bent over and Porter realized she was crying. He walked back to his table and got her a Kleenex and brought it to her, "Now, Miss Haynes, I know this is hard for you to talk about, but you must if you want justice for Ollie."

Schaberg was on his feet before Porter was finished with that sentence shouting, "You honor, he's leading this witness. I object and asked that his last sentence be stricken."

Judge Bickel was nodding in agreement, "Mr. Porter, you will ask questions and not give advice."

Porter ran his hand over his distinctive cleft chin and Bob kicked my leg hard enough for the whole courtroom to hear for that was the other habit Porter had when he was really ready to attack. I turned to look at Bob and his sheepish look and red face made me almost laugh aloud.

"So, Miss Haynes, you and Launie are on top of this building with this horrible scene of destruction playing out in front of you. Who else was with you?"

"Chuck and the other girls."

"Chuck?"

"Yes, sir. He was Launie's driver."

"How long had you known him?"

"A long time. I don't really know to tell the truth, but I had known him since he was a little boy and when we were up there on that roof, he must have been about twenty-one or so."

"Don't you think that is young to be somebody's driver?"

Schaberg stood to object, but Bickel slammed his gavel on the hard oak block on the desk in front of him and almost hissed, "Mr. Porter, I will not warn you again."

Porter looked startled and stopped. He wondered what he had said that Bickel found objectionable. "I don't understand, Your Honor, I was just asking her a question?"

"Proceed, Mr. Porter, but proceed with care, Sir."

"Miss Haynes, who were these other girls with you?"

"We all worked at Launie's place."

"Can you describe Launie's place and what you did?" Porter glanced at the judge.

"We entertained the men who came to drink and watch us dance."

"What kind of dancing did you do?"

She looked down and we could all see she was struggling to use the right words. She looked up and then on up higher until she was staring at the ceiling or even above that like she was asking a higher power than herself to help her with the words.

"We all had our little routines…or acts…that we did over and over every day six days a week. If one of the men acted really interested in our routine, we were to invite him to have drinks with us as we talked."

"You had drinks with the customers?"

Schaberg was on his feet, but Porter cut him off, "You didn't drink while you were working, did you?"

"No, sir. We talked and joked with them and encouraged them to have another drink…"

"Did all those girls come to Fort Walton Beach when Launie opened her new business out on Santa Rosa Boulevard next to the Sound?"

"Yes, sir."

"But, Miss Haynes, you haven't told us how you met Ollie. By the way, do you know Ollie's last name?"

"I didn't then, but he told me much later."

"And what was it?"

She started shaking and crying uncontrollably.

"Your Honor," Porter almost pleaded, "Would you allow a recess until after lunch?"

Even as strict and controlling as Bickel was, somewhere in his being he had compassion on the young woman on the witness stand or he had another reason, so he called a recess.

As Bob and I sat at the IHop and ate pancakes with eggs and sausage for lunch which we both knew we certainly shouldn't be eating, Bob sat talking in a monologue (a habit he has) about the morning's happening. He laughed as he expounded on nearly getting his big butt kicked out of court.

"I've known Judge Bickel all his life. We used to tease the shit out of him about his love for the accordion. He would play that 'squeeze-box' for hours sitting down in front of the library which was just about his only hang out. I don't remember any friends he ever had and when he went off to the University of Miami for law school, we were pretty amazed.

We were really surprised when he came back to town after eight or nine years with a beautiful wife and ran for County Judge. She must have had a bundle because they live in a mansion. But, why do you think that girl got so upset when Porter asked her Ollie's last name?

"I don't know but we better get going cause it going to start again."

The rest of the afternoon was filled with Porter asking how they got to Fort Walton Beach and what they had done before Launie had finally got a license to open her place on the Sound at the east end of Santa Rosa Blvd.

He never did get around to asking Ester Haynes what Ollie's last name was.

I had a really hard time staying awake for I had 'stumbled' out of bed really early this morning, must have been around five o'clock, because I wanted to get away and walk my use-to-be regular walk on the beach.

As I had come around the corner of the Pelican on the walk that runs parallel to the perimeter wall that surrounds the La Mancha, I saw Walkin Al going across the parking lot on his way back to Sea Oats, I guess, for that's where he lives.

I walked on down the boardwalk to the gazebo and stopped for a minute to see how the water was this morning.

A strong scent of a cheap perfume filled the air, at least it smelled cheap to me. Walkin Al was down here this morning—this early in the morning with a woman?

The afternoon session of court ended with Porter still questioning Ester Haynes and it appeared he would be tomorrow.

11

...if you cannot get rid of the family skeleton, you may as well make it dance

Judge Bickel's family has lived in Okaloosa County longer than Bicycle Bob's but their circumstances were much different than Bob's family. Bickel's dad ran the family funeral home, Grace Land Mortuary, so, of course, Jeffrey took a lot of teasing when he was in elementary and middle school about dead people and bodies and Frankenstein.

When he was in the 7th Grade, Bobby Bakersfield had dressed up for Halloween to look just like Jeffrey did most every day. The Bickels couldn't afford many clothes for their eleven children so many of the younger ones wore hand-me-downs. Jeffrey was number nine—three from the youngest—so kids at school might remember from the year before that one of his brothers had worn what he was now wearing. Bobby Bakersfield was persistent and cruel in leading his bunch of buddies as they teased Jeffrey and from those teasing days, Bickel promised himself he would get even.

By the time he was in Choctaw High School, Jeffrey created his own reason for the crowd to tease him. He played the accordion and it became a part of his daily routine to sit somewhere on Choctaw's campus and play what the other guys called 'the squeeze box.' He carried that nickname, Ol Jeffrey Squeeze Box, with him until he graduated with the highest grade point average in his class and left for the University of Miami.

Nobody, but nobody, in the Panhandle goes to the University of Miami so Jeffrey did not return home for holidays and vacations because now there would be another reason for the guys to taunt and mark him as an outsider. But when he finished his Master's and Law Degrees with highest honors he returned to Fort Walton Beach. He had met Diana his wife in Miami and they were now on their way to another large Bickel family for they lived on the shore of Choctawhatchee Bay on Yacht Club Parkway in what anyone would call a mansion with their seven children.

Jeffrey enjoyed seeing the gates to his drive open every morning as he pulled up and pressed the button so his new Lincoln MKS could cruise through. He carefully guided the luxury car through the streets of Fort Walton Beach like a grand old lady even at the height of the tourist season. One of his greatest pleasures was seeing one of the old bunch who had treated him so cruelly, especially if it was Bobbie Bakersfield.

His wife Diana had grown tired of the little town experience of Fort Walton Beach, that and because she suspected him of being unfaithful to her she had taken the children back to her father's big $40M mansion on Hibiscus Island overlooking the MacArthur Causeway in Miami.

He hadn't been cheating on her, but now he was with a most unlikely woman.

When Bob hit the bridge abutment and almost killed himself that night several years ago, Judge Bickel saw it as an opportunity to rub the 'sore' place between the two of them. He visited Bob in the hospital the first chance he could after Bob was allowed to have visitors.

As he walked into Bob's hospital room carrying a Choctaw High stuffed Indian and a pot of flowers he was pleased to see Bob's surprised expression. He stayed way too long knowing it must have been a torment for Bob to have to carry on a conversation with him. When he finally was leaving, he promised to come back soon and asked if he could bring Bob anything. Bob assured him that he didn't need anything and as Jeffrey walked down the hall, he thought he heard Bob cussing. He smiled and walked out to his car as he wondered when and where he might get more revenge on Bob.

He was deliberately dragging out this silly murder trial. He and everyone else knew she was guilty and he was getting tired of the long drawn out shenanigans that Schaberg and Porter were pulling. But he knew his afternoon meetings would come to an end when the trial was over, so he did everything to draw out the proceedings.

He saw Bob and that retired teacher head out the door together for lunch he supposed. Somehow, he thought, this afternoon he would put Bobby Bakersfield out of his court room.

He didn't eat lunch but headed straight for the condo that he thought no one knew about. She was waiting for him and gave him the pleasure of undressing her and carrying her to the bed. She was much younger than his fifty something years but she aroused a desire in him that he had as a young man because she was so young and because she was so forbidden.

They had laughed early on in their meetings for he knew her father and also knew her father would end his making love forever if he found out about them. It hadn't stopped their frequent meetings during the last few months. He was totally fascinated by her look of innocence because he knew her ferocious ability to fight for what she wanted. She was the youngest of her family and she had always got what she wanted. What she had done during the last few weeks for him convinced him he should chance the danger. He laughed to himself that he might be in love, but knew it was just lust.

Upon his return to court, Mr. Porter asked for a meeting with Schaberg at the bench. Porter threw a bombshell that his two eye witnesses were missing from the house he had them living in. Bickel acted like he was furious at another delay, but finally allowed over Schaberg's objection that court would resume in the morning.

12

Ollie

Bob said he would drive us to the courthouse today. I will have some kind of excuse to never do that again for he doesn't drive; he herds.

I followed my routine of getting up very early and taking my walk. I approached the gazebo and saw a figure sitting in the back corner on the bench which runs along that end. "What in the world are you doing down here Al? Didn't I see you yesterday leaving here when I was coming down? Why are you walking in the mornings instead of the late afternoons when you get to see the sunsets? You always talk about walking to see the sunsets?"

"No reason. I just can't sleep much the last few days. So, I get up and walk down here and sit. You are right, the sunrises can't be explained with words. Sunsets are great, but sunrises are really special."

I agreed and went on down the ramp, took off my shoes, and the cold sand awakened every nerve in my body. I'm certain I smelled that perfume again and it wasn't something Al would be wearing.

I walked west and forty minutes later even though I had walked less than a mile, I turned and the sun burst over the horizon at Destin filled with colors that no artist could copy. Great banks of cumulus clouds arose thousands of feet forming a tower the meteorologists call cumulonimbus with their bottoms touched with a rose color that would look so fake if a human attempted to paint the scene but their dark, almost black, main mass foreshadows thunderstorms for the day.

I returned back to the La Mancha beachfront much faster than the trip west and hurried up the ramp of the gazebo and turned on the sidewalk which runs along the end of the Pelican. I sensed an ominous quality in the air but when I saw Jonathan L sitting calmly on his perch, I laughed at myself. As I past the sea oat I had planted there by the wall I felt the feeling of dread leave and I even looked forward to another day in Judge Bickel's courtroom.

Bob pulled up in front of the Pelican in his white BMW and I took a ride from Hell that I will never do again. We arrived at the court house, went through the metal detector, and was in the court room when Judge Bickel walked into the room through the door behind his high bench.

"Court is in session, Gentlemen. And…. let me remind you this is a trial for the murder of one 'Ollie' and nothing else. Mark my words now, I will not stand for any gobbledygook today. You may proceed Mr. Porter."

"Your Honor, I call Miss Ester Haynes back to the witness chair."

The Clerk had Ester reaffirm her oath to tell the truth to all she testified about and court was ready to begin.

As Porter approached her, she sat with her head down, her body shuddered with a hurt inside her that she had had for months after Ollie's death. She trembled as Porter walked toward her because she knew what she would tell the court would make them think Ollie was a monster. As Porter came to where she sat, she escaped--her mind left the place and she went back to a time of love, lust, and happiness.

Ollie was propped up on one elbow next to her leaning over her nude body with a look of satisfaction she had never seen. He told her that night that he had seen what they had done through a thousand keyholes in the dump he was born in, but never in his wildest imagination had he thought of the pleasure those Johns had had. Then he had wanted to do it all over again and this time it was slow and quiet and noiseless and she had loved it. That was the first night in early June and the beginning of a long summer of bliss for the two of them.

Launie always sent one of the girls to get Ollie's food. For some reason Launie didn't want any of the local people to know that Ollie existed. He sat behind a screen at the Library and when a customer got out of control, he would feel Ollie's powerful hand pushing him toward the door. Of course, some locals did visit Launie's place but the main customers were from all over the South usually far away from Fort Walton Beach. If a rowdy customer turned to confront Ollie, all he had to do was turn and see Ollie and then he went quietly. Ollie wasn't particularly tall but he would make Adonis blush at his physique.

Usually the girls would get his food at the Tides Inn up across Highway 98 or at the steak house just around the corner, and Ester now made it a point to be the one to go so she could take it to Ollie in his little room behind the Dorm where the girls lived.

No one ever questioned her about the amount of time she spent with Ollie. Launie probably didn't even know about it and probably wouldn't have cared anyway for her mind was on making money and get the 'fix' she so desperately needed those days. The other girls finally started teasing her about her 'man' but Ester just called them jealous.

She missed her period almost exactly a month after they were together the first time. She was terrified at first, but Ollie was ecstatic with pride. He was so happy that he was going to be a dad and said he wished Old Mitch, the man who had taught him to read and that had taken him to get a birth certificate that had his own last name on it, could see him now.

He had teased her many times that she wouldn't go with him in his enclosure behind his room and lie in the sun nude. They were there wrapped in each other's arms when she had told him he was to be a father. He was so happy that he was laughing like a child, but he quickly said he

57

had to leave and she was suddenly afraid he meant forever. He hushed her with a kiss and said he had to go to the bank over on Beal Parkway to fix his account. He promised with all his heart he loved her and wanted to marry her.

Then two or three days later, Launie had sent him on a trip up the sandy beach on the Island to look for a package. That's when their dream dissolved into a nightmare and finally Ollie's death. He had been so afraid and shaking when they finally returned. She had held him for a long time before he would tell her that a dog had tried to break loose on a balcony and attack him.

She had sung a simple little song to him as she tried to quieten him and finally he had said, "Our son will love that song."

But that hadn't stopped him from going out so early that morning dressed in his Green Arrow outfit and night goggles and wreaking havoc at the La Mancha.

"Miss Haynes? Miss Haynes?" Porter was saying.

Ester blushed red and apologized for not answering, "I'm sorry, Mr. Porter, but I was thinking back."

"Yes, that's where I want you to take us. When did you first meet Ollie?"

"We were on top of that building peering over the edge looking at the filthy water rushing toward us for Katrina had busted through the levees, and… and… he came around a corner from Esplanade Street with a pack of dogs chasing him."

She started shaking again, and Porter got her a glass of water.

"Can you go on, Miss Haynes?"

"I'm sorry... Yes. Just as he jumped for the fire escape, one of the dogs lunged toward him jumping up and it bit down on his calf tearing a big gash in it. It's a big jagged scar that I've seen many times since. That's why he was so terrified of dogs. That's why he went on that rampage down Santa Rosa Blvd... last summer." She paused and quickly looked around to see if anyone had caught her mistake.

She hurried on, "He kicked the High Yeller one still biting down on his calf with his other foot and broke loose from it. He climbed on up and we pulled him as he got close enough and he tumbled over the parapet right... right in front of Launie's feet. He had a big bag of food he had taken from *Lil Dizzy's* and that food was about all we had for three days until a helicopter saw us and got us down from there."

"Weren't you all afraid that Ollie's injured leg would get infected?"

"One of the girls, Kitty, had thought to bring the medicine case with her as we ran away from the water. It had penicillin in it and we gave Ollie shots in his thigh."

"Miss Haynes, I would ask you why you all had penicillin at the place where you all worked, but I better not."

Bickel smiled.

"And then what happened?"

"We were at the Super Dome for several days until Launie rented two U-Carrie vehicles that hauled all of us and we took off for somewhere. We ended up in the parking lot at Walmart in Fort Walton Beach. Launie had just as much money it seemed as she use to have in New Orleans--a lot of money--and took care of us until she bought that place out on the Sound and named it *Launie's Gentlemen's Library.*"

Ester glanced at Launie who was glaring at her as laughter burst out in the courtroom and Bob was by far the loudest. Judge Bickel pounded his gavel on the block on his desk and warned the whole courtroom, while looking straight at Bob, that he would clear the whole damn room if there wasn't order immediately.

"So that's how you came to be on Okaloosa Island?"

"Yes… We were here until…" She finally broke down and could, or would not say another word.

"Can you just answer Yes or No, Miss Haynes?"

She shook her head affirmatively.

"You were here until after Ollie's death and funeral?"

She shook her head up and down with little jerks, whispered "Yes," and collapsed onto the floor.

JC Blevins was the first one to reach her. He lifted her up and laid her out of the defense table.

Judge Bickel recessed court until the following day.

13

Bickel in Control

Before court began the next day, Judge Bickel came into the court room and stood in front of the room announcing, "Ladies and gentlemen in this room, I want you to very carefully listen to what I am about to say. There will be no more talking, responding out loud, or disruption in this courtroom. I will empty all people, including future witnesses until they are called, and we will have a little private trial. Does anyone need this repeated?"

I involuntarily started to look to my right to see Bob's reaction but remembered that it was Wednesday and he was not in the courtroom today but out in the Gulf fishing.

"Okay, then, let's resume, Mr. Porter."

Curtis Porter asked for Ester to return to the witness chair.

I guess I had not really looked at her closely before. She was probably in her middle thirties but looked quite a bit younger. Her figure would make most women jealous and even an old retired teacher like me could see that her legs were her best asset. They were muscular and firm from dancing so much, I guessed. For an instant, another pair of legs like hers flashed through my mind but I couldn't place where I had seen them. The other striking thing that made her face appealing were her eyes; they were wide apart and always looked straight at whoever was talking to her, except when she lowered her head to compose herself. As Max our former beach attendant would have said, "Ester Haynes is fine!"

"Miss Haynes, yesterday you were telling us about how you just arrived at Fort Walton Beach and that Launie Sanderson had bought the property out at the east end of Santa Rosa Blvd and opened *Launie's Gentlemen's Library..."*

Laughter erupted in the room and Bickel pounded his gavel. "I have warned you and I will empty this room on the next disruption." He involuntarily looked to where Bob usually sat I noticed.

"Miss Haynes, I apologize for the people in the room and ask you to go on with telling us about the job you had with Miss Sanderson."

Schaberg was on his feet, "That's already been answered, Your Honor..."

"Overruled, I'll take care of what we hear in this court, Mr. Schaberg."

Schaberg looked startled and turn to look at Porter who also was looking at Judge Bickel with a questioning look. The whole courtroom was silent and everyone was looking around wondering what has just happened.

"Continue Mr. Porter."

"Okay, now Miss Haynes... What did the girls do at Miss Sanderson's place?"

She hesitated, "About the same as we had done in New Orleans except toward the end...."

"What do you mean 'toward the end?"

"Well, Launie seemed to lose interest in what we were doing." She looked toward Launie and was met with a stare so steely that she quickly turned back to Porter. "There were lots of days we didn't see or hear from her. She was out on that big boat, the *Lollipop,* a lot of the time."

There were snickers of derision. Bickel who had been looking down at some paper jerked up his head and the courtroom became quiet.

"Kitty, the oldest of us and probably the most outgoing, almost ran the place until she just disappeared one night. And then Chuck disappeared too."

"Chuck disappeared?"

"Yes, they had a big fight… Him and Launie… And then he was just not there anymore."

"How do you know about the fight?"

"Some of us heard Launie cussing and screaming that night. One of the girls knocked on her door and when she didn't open it, one of us did. We all gathered around the doorway and some of us went inside where she was sitting on the floor surrounded by broken glasses and a spilled bottle of something. The table was overturned and looked like it had been slammed against the wall. Her face was all swelled up and turning purple. She was going to have a black eye and did for many days. After that she wore so much eye make-up that you couldn't see her eyes, just the sockets."

"And Chuck was not there?"

"I never saw him again after that."

"And then the same happened with the girl you call Kitty?"

"No, I mean yes, she was gone all of a sudden, but she and Launie didn't have a fight because Launie was very upset and called her a bunch of names because she—Kitty just disappeared. But Kitty was gone a long time before Launie and Chuck had the fight and he left."

Launie Sanderson looked like she would come out of her seat and spat out, "You ungrateful bitch. You will pay for what you say."

Schaberg grabbed Launie's arm, but Porter was fit to be tied, "Your Honor, I call for a mistrial!"

"Oh, come on Mr. Porter, you know very well that is not going to happen, not in my lifetime."

Bickel turned to Schaberg, "Mr. Schaberg, if you cannot control your client, I will put her in that soundproof glass cage back there so we cannot hear anything else she might say to disrupt these proceedings. Continue, Mr. Porter."

Porter looked in Schaberg's direction and I thought I saw a slight smile as he rubbed his hand across his chin. "Miss Haynes, I had just asked you when the woman known as 'Kitty' had disappeared before we were interrupted."

"Early in the summer, I think…June or early July. Some weird guy was coming in regularly and asking only for her. After she did her routine right in front of him, they would sit and he would drink and she would keep the drinks coming. I saw her leave with him one night."

That pair of legs I had thought about a few minutes before suddenly were attached to that first body on the beach last year and I almost caused a disruption in the court as I thought I knew who it was.

"Now, Miss Haynes, you said Miss Sanderson was not paying much attention to you girls?"

"Just before the end…"

"The end?"

"Before Ollie's death," Ester was crying again "before his murder." She sat and sobbed uncontrollably for a few minutes until Porter started again.

"Miss Haynes, I am almost finished asking you questions. Will you try to answer just a few more? Okay, now we know you and Ollie were spending quite a bit of time together, and that people could see that you were going to have a baby. Had you and Ollie talked about any plans?"

"That was all ruined, of course when he…" It seemed like minutes as she struggled to get the words out, "Yes. We were going to just disappear like Chuck and Kitty had. We were going to go two nights after…" The next came out of her like a scream, "…two nights after Launie Sanderson took him out and shot him the back of his head!"

The room was in an uproar again at hearing those words. Bickel was pounding his gavel furiously and everyone was talking amongst themselves.

Ester Haynes' face suddenly went blank. She was crying hysterically and saying, "That's when my world ended. That's when I lost him. Oh God that I could have died with him…no, no I was going to have Mitch…I had to live."

She disappeared back into her thoughts, thoughts of that day when she and the other girls stood around Ollie's new dug grave and they all laid the beer can medallions around the stone they had bought for him. How someone had given her a stack of money and she had bought her ticket to Memphis. How Memphis had been a living hell for her as she had Little Mitch in a dump of a motel with two of the other girls helping her with the birth. How she had finally said good-bye to the others and returned to Fort Walton Beach. How Fort Walton Beach had been little better than Memphis except she had a job, little Mitch, and a place to sit close to where Ollie lay.

And then another time came to mind; they were like little children as they dug into the bank of one of the drain-off spaces that are along Santa Rosa Blvd to drain rainwater down into the Sound. She had been amazed at the trove of things Ollie had hidden there. He said, "My hero had a special cave for his equipment, so I had to find a place also. It took a long time to build my cave because it kept falling in so I put all these rocks in here. I kept thinking that the utility men would find it and destroy all my things or that some kids would find it and tell their folks."

They had taken all his bows and arrows and the many articles the might belong to the Green Arrow of Ollie's imagination back to Ollie's room. It had taken them two night to finish the mission as he called it and they had laughed like high school kids pulling a prank as they smuggled in his treasures.

She guessed they had burned in the mysterious fire that burned Launie's place right after Ollie was killed.

He had marveled when the baby had kicked him one night as they snuggled together and had laid his head on her stomach as the baby continued to kick. He had talked to the baby and called him Mitch and promised to make a good life for him. She had stopped him in midsentence when she had asked, "What if it is a girl?" He hadn't even flinched as he replied, "Then she will be beautiful like her mother and I will take her to get ice cream and I will dance with her when she is homecoming queen and I will chase no-account boys away. They had laughed for minutes.

"But a homecoming queen can't have parents who aren't married to each other, so let's figure out how to get married," he had said. She had sobbed on his chest for five minutes or so before he could convince her to tell what was wrong? Finally she said, "Maybe we'd better wait until we leave here because Launie might try to stop us."

"No, I'm going to find out tomorrow and we're going to do it, that is, if you will marry me?"

Then she had laughed and laughed and he thought at first she was laughing at him but when she made it clear that he was silly for that for she would be the happiest woman around if they were married, then he had laughed too.

The next morning they had gone to the courthouse and presented their birth certificates and were told they would have to wait three days after their blood test came back to get a license; Ollie was furious and as they went back to the Dorm on the city bus, he had blurted out, "What if we don't live that long?"

Ester slid out of the chair and landed in the floor.

Schaberg was shouting that her last statement should be stricken.

Judge Bickel was pounding his gavel with sharp fast bangs.

J C Blevins rushed forward to tend to Ester Haynes.

I looked Launie Sanderson squarely in the face and she sat with a wide smile but smile turned to a vulgar snarl as she looked squarely at me.

Bickel finally recessed court.

Bob had missed what turned out to be the most exciting day in court in months.

14

Men are deceivers ever....

During the whole summer, Craig and his crew tried to catch that darn cat; the swiftest and youngest of the crew, AJ, suffered a deep bite from reaching under a beach sunflower vine where Poseidon sat with his back to the fence so he couldn't be ambushed. Because of the presence of the cat, Bette had persuaded a doctor in town to issue rabies vaccine solutions to Barry and Diana Page who are new residents that live up next to Don and Shirley Herd in the Sea Turtle building. They are both registered nurses and Diana was quick on the scene when Poseidon bit AJ. She cleaned his wound and gave him the first of the shots.

AJ is new to the La Mancha this season and appears to be a dependable concerned young man who is always polite and friendly whenever someone speaks to him. He moves from job to job with an assurance that the man he replaced didn't seem to have. If AJ has one habit that I dislike is his going gung-ho in the golf cart with his left leg dandling out the side. I had a buddy who hit a bump doing that and tore his ankle in several places, so I cringe every morning as I see AJ arrive at work at exactly seven o'clock and go whizzing up the sidewalk in the golf cart to start cleaning the pool.

On either side of the pool where the sidewalks intersect from the Pelican on one side and the Dolphin on the other with the boardwalk that leads down to the gazebo, there is a circle of pavement large enough to hold a barbeque pit and a concrete picnic table.

AJ finishes the pool and away he goes in the cart to empty the trash and use the leaf blower to clean the picnic areas. On the morning he was bit, he was blowing the creeping sun flower vine back against the perimeter wall as it was taking over part of the lawn. That vine survives so well because the water from the beach shower where almost everyone stops to wash the sand off, drains right down to where the vine grows.

Craig has let one of the sunflower vines grow up over the wall at a spot close to where I sit on the wall and not too far from the grill close to the boardwalk. Beach sunflowers would not be recognizable to people from Kansas as they are so different than the big bold blossoms of the sunflowers there. Van Gogh would probably not be interested in painting them either for they are more like a daisy than our perception of a sunflower. They grow close to the ground in bushes that are covered with the bright yellow flowers.

A J must have seen some bit of trash of something for he reached into the vine not knowing that Poseidon was hunched under there as he had been eating what some careless picnickers had left the night before. Poseidon clamped down on AJ's hand; AJ screamed in pain, and Poseidon dashed across the lawn to disappear into the Air Command property.

As if from out of nowhere, Reverend Levi Crabtree was standing where the sidewalks intersect shouting at the top of his lungs, "Evil will fall from the sky and they shall be destroyed for their wrongs. They will burn in hell for their misdoings and shall shrivel into nothing because they have let the land be filled with whores and heathens."

I was in my usual place on my balcony drinking my coffee, Craig and AJ were huddled together looking at AJ's hand, Bicycle Bob had peddled up and all of us were staring at the Reverend in total silence.

He turned and looked up at me, "And those who report the lies of the wicked are just as wicked," He snarled.

"What the Hell?" Bob hollered at him. "What do you think you are doing? Get away from here with all those people watching and hearing you. Damn it to Hell, you will ruin all our business."

69

Bob lowered his bicycle onto the ground and stepped toward Crabtree which is very unusual for Bob seldom dismounts from his bicycle when he is out and about. When he was right in the little man's face he lowered his voice and talked to Crabtree for some time. We couldn't hear what he was saying, but Crabtree kept retreating from Bob. Bob must have talked to him for four or five minutes when he finally said, "You are a menace which we do not need here and I want you to quit your everlasting shouting. Get the Hell away from here." Crabtree started to say something, but Bob took a step toward him, and Crabtree retreated down the sidewalk and around the corner of the Pelican.

Diana Page appeared, cleaned AJ's wound, and before he could object very much gave him the first in a series of rabies shots. He would be doing light work around the La Mancha for some time.

After that, Craig was persistent that Poseidon be caught so large wire traps were placed around La Mancha late at night and taken in before guests got up in the morning. One night a coyote went after the rotisserie chicken piece in one of the traps and the Game and Wildlife man had to come get it to take out in the forest north of town. The crew found several traps that were a tangled mass of wires and frames—trying to catch Poseidon with a wire trap was like going after a Great White with an aluminum cage.

Worse than anything else though were the gulls; they swooped in and grabbed pieces of chicken fighting and shrieking and knocking into each other in midflight. The final straw happened the night a skunk went after the same bait and liberally spraying that horrible powerful stink that lingered all the next day. The trap idea was abandoned.

We seldom saw Poseidon during the day after AJ was bit, but I saw him almost every morning just before dawn as I left the Pelican to walk the beach. I suppose I should have been afraid of him but he never made any move that he meant me harm. I don't know what I would have done if he had attacked me though. Everyone who lives at the La Mancha knows I walk west on the beach every morning and turn just at the right time so I see the sunrise over the horizon at Destin six miles to the east so if Poseidon had attacked me, someone would find me before I suffered too long.

I usually saw him sitting in the same place just on the other side of the ugly chain-link fence; the boundary between us and the Air Command. At one point there is a piece of the fence that looks like it's been cut from the top down about six feet. A big hole hangs open there.

We had wondered since he suddenly appeared what he was eating. Henry Embser, the beach attendant was accused of bringing food with him to feed the cat. Craig even went so far as to inspect Henry's car several times randomly as he entered the property at the guard house, but never found any food except Henry's lunches. Being the likeable guy he is, Henry laughed at Craig the first few times he was searched, but on about the fourth time, he was adamant that he was not feeding Poseidon and told Craig to leave him alone.

Bob and I had teased Gladis about feeding the cat since she lives in the closest condo to the fence, but she promised that it was not her.

Craig had the security people patrol the property more times at night to try to find out how Poseidon was surviving. Somehow, no one ever caught Reverend Crabtree as he regularly fed that cat. So Poseidon flourished and it was a mystery to all of us how. Getting water was no problem for the sprinklers came on early each morning and left puddles of water close enough to the fence for him to get water.

Bette was very concerned about Poseidon as she feared he might scare or injure a guest or one of us who live here or another employee, so she contacted Eglin to see if they would get rid of the cat. We saw a few Air Force grunts walk the area a few times but they never found him.

But Bette had much bigger problems that she didn't know about but would very soon.

15

The House on Tarpon Drive

It's a paradox that is very difficult to describe. From the outside, it really looks like a crystal that has been unearthed and is standing on its end. The dirt and sand have been polished clean as it stands stark white, whiter than the buildings of the La Mancha, with its bright copper roof that catches the rays of both the sunrise and sunset. It has be a fake copper because it has not oxidized in our salty air. Sharp pointy pyramids jut up in four different places and at the very top and between them is a mesa— anyone from the Southwest would recognize it as a mesa from a distance.

The house sits at the closest point to the Sound on Tarpon Drive; all the streets on the Sound side of the Island are really semicircular streets that exit Santa Rosa Blvd and wind around and reenter the Blvd further on. They all have names of different kinds of fish. It certainly is not a beach house, in fact, you could imagine it in a science fiction scene on some alien planet. It appears to be three stories tall but it's hard to tell that for there are windows scattered here and there in no particular pattern except near the top of the mesa is a row of windows which are totally an oxymoron to this paradox. They appear to be Northern African, Egyptian or Moorish, in shape and they are opaque. They face east and I suppose that Brooks Bridge can be seen from them, if indeed, anything can be seen through them. They may be opaque to stop the bright sun as it comes up over Choctawhatchee Bay or they may just be an architectural element. To me they are like putting stained-glass windows in a log cabin for they do not 'match' in any way the feeling or form of the house.

The drive off Tarpon Drive up to what should be the front door is beautifully laid with cobble pavers which look like river rocks and at one point another path breaks away from the main one and circles down around the west side of the house. There is no front door to the house but there is a button to push that is almost concealed in the frame of what turns out to be an elevator. Even the button is nearly lost in the bright chipped glass pieces of the elevator's opening. It's as if no one is welcome here and anyone who must come, must be invited.

The only visitors I have ever seen at the house as I walk up Santa Rose Blvd to the Thumb for a fruit bar are delivery trucks. Frequently, the brown truck stops there, the driver pushes the button on the elevator as I suppose he it found long ago and then he leaves. I have actually stood and waited a couple of times for someone to open the elevator door and get the package but no one ever has as I stand there.

From the Sound, the house is just as mysterious. What appears to be the top two floors are completely glass framed irregularly in squares, some really big squares and some as small as six or eight inches. Almost all the squares are opaque, just like the strange windows on the mesa in front, with only a few small squares having glass. It is on the west side so I guess it is logical to shut out the direct rays of the setting sun if indeed you can see out of those opaque squares. Several times I have seen the sunset reflected on the house as Bob and I go up the Sound in his fishing boat, *The Choctaw Pride*.

Spanning across the back yard is a concrete wall that is about fifteen feet high and thick enough for a person to walk across the top. It almost hides the entire bottom level of the house and has a dock within it for a boat.

Bob and I were talking the other night as we sat on his balcony eating my Uncle Robert's Albuquerque Steak, a huge thick sirloin marinated in red wine and many spices, and I saw the bright copper metal roof of the house, "Have you ever been in that big house on Tarpon."

"Once a long time ago," he said as he took a big slurp on the straw sticking in his White Russian, "Got invited to a drunken party one night."

"What's it like on the inside?"

"About as weird as it is on the outside. There's really only two floors in the place. The bottom two levels you see from the outside are just a big vaulted room that has an electric door which opens to let a boat in and out. Think of a vault and that's about it."

"You're putting me on, right?"

"Nope. You ride the elevator up to the top level and that's the only place that has anything that looks like a home. One the ride up you can see through the little port hole of a window in the elevator door the interior of the other side of the house. There's a circular stairs that hugs the wall and goes through a trap door up to the floor above."

"The west view is just the Sound and I guess the new jail now. The east view is something though as you can see Destin and the sunrise must be beautiful from there. Brooks Bridge is almost centered in that string of windows."

"What in the world are those windows?"

"Damned if I know. They are pointed at the top. You being the wiseass you are at times would probably called them Gothic. Why you interested in that house all of a sudden?"

"No reason, I walk by it sometimes and just wonder about it."

"Must have cost a pretty penny to build that thing."

But then we were talking about a very large sail boat going by on the Sound and Bob said, "Damned idiot has his motor running. Doesn't have any sense. And local person would know the tide would pulled that thing through the Sound and clear through the Bay just as fast as he's going with his motor running."

An ambulance went screaming east through Fort Walton Beach and we saw its flashing lights as it crossed Brooks Bridge.

As it went, I got a glimpse of the copper roof of that house.

We didn't know it then, of course, but Bob would visit that house again in the near future.

16

Old Sam

When I take Skipper walking, he seems to eagerly wait for Lewis to appear with Old Sam; a best buddy dog just as many times with humans is usually as different as day is to night. Skipper, Josephine Jones' feisty little Corgi that has come to live with me after Josephine's death is about as tame as a baby otter. He runs around dragging his chest and belly in the high grass and often chasing his stubby little tail. Sam is undoubtedly the most familiar dog around the La Mancha. Lewis and Sally Smyth don't know just how old he as they got him from a shelter after Katrina left so many pets homeless across the southern borders of five states in 2005. When he first arrived at the La Mancha he was a beautiful almost red Golden Retriever who longed it seemed to run free, but ten years later Sam has trouble even walking.

Sam and Skipper became friends on the elevator. There was little room for them to 'sniff' each other that morning Skipper had moved into the Pelican from the Dolphin where Josephine had lived because Lewis and I were with them but it started a life-long friendship for them.

Afterward when I would take Skipper on the elevator he would sniff the floor and corners and whine. I wondered why until one day the elevator opened on our third floor and Lewis and Sam were already on for they live up on the sixth floor. The two dogs acted like long lost friends. Skipper was jumping and barking and Sam was actually wagging his tail and smiling.

Lewis said Sam always whined and seemed to be looking for his friend when they rode down without us. We didn't realize it then, but Skipper would be whining with no reward very soon.

The La Mancha is the oldest of the condo complexes down Santa Rosa Blvd but the buildings at the La Mancha are undoubtedly the strongest. Think of them as reinforced concrete boxes stacked together with a firewall in between each two condos; they aren't really separated as the thick floors were poured in long slabs with five condos on each end with the elevators attached in center of each. Perhaps the weak link in the La Mancha is the plumbing because forty years ago when some of the buildings were constructed plumping equipment was primitive to what we have today. Many of the water pipes are made of iron and installation required large holes be cut through the concrete to get the stiff iron pipes through to the neighboring condo.

Bette had hired and instructed several plumbers from Fort Walton Beach and Destin to 'fix' problems in several of the buildings and on several floors of those buildings, so this, along with the havoc once again on our beach, was the summer of fixing the plumbing.

The Pelican was one of the buildings needing the most repairs even though it was the second newest of the six buildings. We listened all summer starting at 9 o'clock in the mornings to jack hammers as they pounded their way through thick concrete slabs or walls so new pipes could be installed. Therefore, there were many 'holes' throughout the building from one condo to another and one floor to another that have been filled in from the repairs.

*

Fall had turned the hot sticky days of July and August into cool autumn breezes and nights when sliding doors to balconies could be left open. Lewis and Sally left their screen door to their sixth floor condo open so Sam could have the run of the balcony where he slept almost every night.

*

She stretched as high as she could, so high her rib bones were showing along her sides. She felt the cool breeze as it came into the opening at the top of her cage. Someone had has made a horrible mistake as the latch on top had not been fastened; it snapped open as she pushed against it and she pulled up and began to slither through it. After more of her was on the floor than in the cage the rest of her long thick body gained speed as it fell to the floor and finally her tail flipped out over the rim of the cage and the rattles chattered as she coiled on the cool tile.

She flicked her forked tongue to get some bearing as she felt the breeze as it came though the opening around the water pipe. She pulled herself across the Saltillo tiles toward the opening covering four of the eighteen inch tiles when she was fully extended across the floor. Somehow, the diamond markings on her thick body complimented the diamond patterns of the tiles.

She started through the hole sensing that danger awaited on the other end but her primal urge to not be out in the open urged her on. Sam had heard the noise in the pipe and as he sniffed the air, he sense the danger coming toward him. His natural instinct to protect his family filled him with a courage he hadn't felt for a long time. He stationed himself directly in front of the hole. She hesitated for a moment and then moved her head and several inches of her body through the opening. Sam pounced on her grabbing her behind her flat thick head. His aim was not the best as he had caught her down on her body. She struck at him and sank her fangs into the fur on his throat. He yelped and turned lose only to lunge in again and this time his aim and bite were much better. Whacking her against furniture and the tile floor he soon had pulled her out the door onto his balcony.

The struggle and crashing of their bodies awoke Sally first. As she turned on a light in the living room, she saw the monstrous snake rear its head back and strike into Sam for the last time. She screamed as she saw the snake sank its fangs into the tender part of Sam's thigh where his leg attached to the rest of his body. By this time, Lewis was standing in the balcony door amazed and terrified at the huge snake. Sam, with a final burst of energy, went head first into the stone railing of the balcony. The snake was knocked loose and went hurling through the air to land six floors below.

Lewis hurriedly called security to tell Gerald that a rattlesnake had attacked Sam and was loose on the ground at the Pelican in front of the parking lot. It took several minutes to persuade Gerald that he was serious. As she knelt on the floor of the balcony holding Sam's head in her arms and rocking back and for crying, Sally was on her phone calling 911 at the same time telling the dispatcher that a rattlesnake had killed her dog and was loose on the grounds at the La Mancha.

*

She turned and twisted on the ground jerking and rolling like snakes do when they are hurt. Her underbelly could be seen in the light of the street light in the parking lot as she turned and turned in her pain. Hands in heavy leather gloves reached out and a forked rod came down behind her head and she was forced to stop struggling. The hand picked her up and dropped her into an Igloo Cooler.

*

When Gerald finally arrived with a deputy from the police department, there was no evidence that anything had happened there on the ground beneath Lewis and Sally's condo. The deputy searched their apartment and saw that there had been a struggle and that Old Sam lay on the balcony dead.

Bette was almost hysterical the next morning, "What if that thing had bit a guest. We would be ruined, sued for millions." She had both of

Reverend Levi Crabtree's condos searched but nothing was found in either. She also thought she should call that doctor to see if he would issue snake venom antidote to the Pages now that a deadly snake was loose at the La Mancha.

The snake was in the trunk of Crabtree's big black Pontiac in the cooler.

Crabtree had called attention to himself and the three women, not just as a loud-mouthed diversion, but as a potential danger which was not acceptable to someone.

17

Someone Knows How This Will End

Before anyone was allowed into the courtroom the morning the trial was reconvened after the Labor Day weekend, Judge Bickel call Porter and Schaberg into his quarters, a little room with no windows which was directly behind the platform which elevated his desk above the rest of the courtroom.

"Gentlemen, it's time we pause and discuss a few things. First of all, I will not tolerate from either of you any more of this petty squabbling which has drawn this trial out far too long."

The two lawyers looked at each other knowing that Bickel himself was the one dragging out the trial with his recessing the proceedings frequently and his personal business on many afternoons but they said nothing.

"Mr. Porter, I want to know right now just where you are going with this and how much longer we can expect you to call witnesses. You are costing Okaloosa County a great deal of money. He paused... Well?"

"Oh, I'm sorry Your Honor, I didn't realize you wanted me to interrupt you. I have four more witness, Sam Ripley and Alice Pearl who saw the whole thing and who will be my last witnesses and the other two will take only a few minutes if there are no objections to what they testify about or if unknown things don't come up while they are testifying."

"Mr. Porter, I think I know what you are doing with all your questioning and I am surprised that Mr. Schaberg has not objected more than he has."

"I don't think I know what you mean."

"Bull shit, sir. You are not really trying this trial but preparing the court for what you think will be another more important trial."

"I assure you," as he cleared his throat, "that I had no idea that it would take so long to find one of Launie's girls up in Memphis. You know that didn't even happen but that she was already back in Fort Walton Beach. I had to have time to prepare her for the trial."

"And just what does she have to do with the murder of whoever this Ollie is? All you have done is to show how she worked for Launie Sanderson."

Schaberg started to interrupt but stopped.

Schaberg was one of the three who knew there would be no other trial for he knew that someone was in the courtroom every day who would see that it never happened. He had even told Launie Sanderson the same thing the first time he had been sent to talk with her about the disastrous mess she had caused for the boss down in Miami. She had been warned many times that she was making a spectacle of herself with that big yacht and then with her traipsing around Fort Walton Beach stoned on some kind of drug. No, Miami wouldn't allow it. He had tried to talk the boss down in Miami to get rid of her, but that hadn't happened before she had suddenly killed Ollie. The one thing that Schaberg didn't know was who would stop the proceedings—stop them dead.

Every day he scanned the courtroom for a face which he had seen every day and he kept coming back to the old retired teacher people called the Prof and that clown of a sidekick who always sat beside him. That was a good joke—'side kick,' for Schaberg had seen him kick his friend several times when a serious or outlandish thing happened in the courtroom. But he doubted if either of them were the person for they were both either well respected or a long time resident of Okaloosa Country. So Schaberg started studying the jury one by one until he settled on Juror #4. He checked the records of who the juror was and found that he was not only a resident of the La Mancha but also the Foreman of the jury—Louis Smyth.

He came out of his revelry and acted interested in what the other two were discussing and said, "If that's the case, Judge Bickel, you should deny him what he's doing and stop it."

"You have done very little complaining and objecting, Mr. Schaberg, and that is your job. I know my job and am doing it."

All three of the men were glaring at one another and Bickel knew that he had just opened another can of worms by having this meeting.

"Mr. Porter, how much longer are you going to question Miss Haynes?"

"I am finished with my questions to her, Judge, and ready for Mr. Schaberg to cross-examine her.

18

Bob Gets Kicked Out of Court

When Judge Bickel called the court to order a few minutes later and the jury had been seated, he looked out at the courtroom and then turn to face the jury. He had the clerk call Ester Haynes back to the witness chair.

I didn't know any of the jury except for my friend, Lewis Smyth, Old Sam's owner. Their condo is between the two that most of us thought that rattlesnake had come from. Some of us were still skittish about what had happened to that snake and if it is really dead as Bette and Craig continually assures us. You could frequently here Craig tell some resident that, "Sure that thing is dead. Poseidon killed it." We still weren't too sure about that.

Even though Lewis and his wife Sally have both lived and owned their condo for a long time, they are rather private people and don't sit around the pool and 'gossip' as much as others. I don't mean to imply that Lewis and Sally aren't friendly for they are. And they are very considerate people for Old Sam hadn't been gone for a week until they had two new dogs; a brother and sister set of almost identical red retrievers, named Sam and Missy—magnificent dogs, but they would never be the friend to Skipper that Old Sam had been.

Lewis and Sally's own encounters with the rattlesnake that had killed undoubtedly the most loved dog at the La Mancha had not only terrified them but the whole La Mancha complex. Like Bicycle Bob, Gladis and me, they had told their worry and fears about the snake to Bette. When Sally confronted Bette about what the La Mancha management was going to do about an Eastern Diamond Back loose on the property and Bette had given what was the standard answer that everyone on her staff was looking for it, Sally had gone up to Georgia to stay with Lewis's mother until the snake was found.

Bette appeared just as shocked as anyone else and even called in a 'Snake' man to try to find it, but he left after a couple of unsuccessful days. We saw more of Bette out on 'campus' as I call the grounds at the La Mancha than we ever had—she seemed to be taking more control of the property than ever. She appeared the day after the snake had killed Old Sam in high leather shoes and carrying a 'snake' stick. Craig told her how ridiculous she looked and what attention she was making of herself to the guests so she appeared after lunch looking normal.

Like Bob said one afternoon, "Where the Hell is that snake? It can't just dissolve into thin air. Someone knows and is hiding that damn thing."

Sally had hesitantly returned when we were all told that Poseidon had killed it. Then, again, there was doubt for its body was never found. Craig told everyone, "That cat ate the damn thing."

I see Lewis almost every morning as I am walking and he is taking the two new dogs out for their morning constitution. He and I had not talked about the trial at all since it started months ago except for one time. We met one morning recently as I was coming up the boardwalk from my walk on the beach and Lewis had the dogs and they were walking down the boardwalk toward the gazebo.

We said our good mornings and I leaned down to pet one of the dogs and Lewis said, "I'm so damn tired of this trial that I could just get up and walk out. I bet you are too for you have to be there every day also."

I didn't answer but shook my head affirmatively, "We shouldn't talk about it though."

And I walked on and turned on the sidewalk toward the Pelican.

And just now our eyes met across the courtroom as Judge Bickel said, "This morning I have met with the two attorneys in this case and they assure me that the trial will soon be finished and we can celebrate Thanksgiving knowing we won't have to come back to court on this matter."

It appeared to me that both Porter and Schaberg looked surprised and Bob sure thought something was strange also for he gently nudged my foot.

"Mr. Porter, you may resume you questioning of the witness."

"I have no more questions of this witness, Your Honor."

"Mr. Schaberg, the witness is yours if you have any questions."

Schaberg walked slowly up to the witness chair and stood between it and the jury railing so that Ester would have to look toward them as she testified. He had his back to her and faced the jury as he ask his first question.

"Miss Haynes, what do you do for a living?"

"I work at one of the Winn-Dixie's over on Mary Ester Cutoff."

"And what do you do there?"

"I wait on customers at the check-out and sometimes stock shelves."

"How long have you been working there?"

"Since I came back to Fort Walton Beach."

He whirled around and was almost in her face as he said, "'Came Back?' What do you mean by 'came back?"

Ester wasn't fazed by Schaberg's tactics as Porter had warned her earlier that morning that Schaberg would try to put on a show, "I was gone for a few months after Launie's place was closed down."

I thought I saw an annoyed grimace cross his face when she had answered him so calmly but he continued, "When we were last here, you said that some of you 'girls' heard Launie Sanderson cussing and screaming and that you went to her room to see what was the matter?"

"Yes."

"Did you ever go back to Launie Sanderson's room after she was arrested?"

"No."

He almost strutted a few steps toward the jury and once again turned quickly on Ester, "Now, careful, Miss Haynes... Didn't you girls go back to Launie Sanderson's room, tear open the headboard, open the safe, and take money?"

"No, I did not."

He smiled, "Then how did you get money for the plane ticket to Memphis?"

"From one of the other girls."

He looked amazed, "Oh, you had nothing to do with robbing Launie Sanderson's safe? You had no part in that robbery?"

"No, I did not."

"That is amazing Miss Haynes. Are we to believe that you are just an innocent woman who all of a sudden had the money to pay cash for a same day ticket?"

"Yes, sir. I was sitting down on the little dock back of the Dorm when they took Launie's money."

She was so angry that this time she didn't break down as she spit out, "I was sitting down there because that's where I saw Ollie the last time he was alive. I saw him leave with Launie on the *Lollipop* that night. I saw his joy at riding on that big yacht."

"Oh, come on! Are you asking us to believe that?"

"You are an ass, sir."

Schaberg was furious, but Bickel interrupted, "The jury will ignore Miss Haynes' emotional reply as to what Mr. Schaberg might be.

Giggles filled the room and Bob's was the loudest.

I thought she was going to stand up in the witness chair as she sat up straight and leaned forward, "Wouldn't you have believed me if I said I did take the money?"

The courtroom erupted into loud laughter.

Bickel pounded his gavel.

Finally there was silence.

She impressed us all as she almost hissed, "What you should be asking, Mr. Schaberg, is why in the world was there over $500,000 in that headboard in Launie's bedroom?"

The courtroom went wild at that and it took Bickel several minutes to get control. He nearly spluttered, "I will clear the room if that happens again."

Schaberg looked like a silly sophomore boy with a lame excuse for not having his homework, so he said, "By the way, Miss Haynes, what was Ollie's last name? Mr. Porter seems to have forgotten he promised to find out."

She wasn't about to settle down as she was really angry, "Oh, I think Mr. Porter knew exactly what he was doing, Mr. Schaberg. I think he knew you would be asking me if he didn't and he was right."

Schaberg looked totally shook-up, but quickly turned to the judge, "Your Honor, this witness is apparently hostile to the defense, and I wish the court to declare her so."

"As you wish, Mr. Schaberg, but the court is anxiously awaiting for her to answer your question. Go ahead, Miss Haynes, answer Mr. Schaberg's question and remember I have declared you as a hostile witness to the Defense."

"Ollie's last name was Haynes." She pulled a piece of paper from her purse and waved it in Schaberg's face, "Here is our marriage license with his name on it. We didn't have time to get married because she killed him."

Schaberg looked like he had bite into a bitter Key lime as he headed toward the Defense table.

Whispers and talk broke out again in room. Bob turned to me and forgot where he was and almost shouted, "What the Hell?"

Judge Bickel was slamming his gavel on that piece of hard wood on his desk and the room finally was at order again.

Bickel said with what I thought was way too much pleasure, "Will the Bailiff remove Mr. Bob Bakersfield from the courtroom?"

Bob started to object as Katrina Hart walked over and stood in front of Bob. He slowly stood grunting with a fake pain he sometimes uses to call attention to his injured thigh; the thigh he injured months ago and which doesn't seem to bother him at all as he whizzes around the La Mancha on his bike.

She waited patiently and as he slowly walked toward the back door of the courtroom, she followed closely behind not saying a word and being very quiet.

Katrina Hart was a rookie when Schaberg had first come to see Launie when Launie was arrested for Ollie's death. I, too, wondered how she had kept her job after letting Launie escape, but somehow, she had convinced the Sheriff and had kept her job. She made no mistakes now.

"And now, Mr. Schaberg, you may continue with your hostile witness."

"Your Honor, I have no more questions at this time."

The entire courtroom burst into loud laughter as Judge Bickel once again slammed his gavel and announce that Court was in recess until three that afternoon.

19

More Money

The next afternoon I got a call from the young man who works at my bank over on Beal Parkway who had helped me when that mysterious account with over a million dollars had been deposited in my name last fall and now he had more news.

"Prof, I've been keeping up with the trial and your story in the *NorthWest Daily* this morning made me think that a man who fits the description of the victim came in and changed an account a few days before he was killed. Do you have time to come to the bank and talk?"

"I could come now because the judge recessed court today."

"He does that a lot, doesn't he. How long has this been going on?"

"Over six long months. I'll be over in thirty minutes."

When I arrived at the bank, Justin was waiting for me and took me into one of the little rooms where new accounts were set-up in privacy.

"I wasn't totally open with you on the phone, Prof, because yesterday afternoon a large amount of money was electronically transferred into the account I was telling you about."

"Oh, how much? And from where?"

"You won't believe it but its $50,000 and a bank in Chicago transferred it."

"Good God! Another red Buick account."

"I don't know what you mean, 'red Buick.'"

"Well, late last summer I started getting postcards with a number on them and always a red Buick was somewhere in the picture on the card. I finally figured out that the number might be a back account and that's when you started helping me."

"Oh, I see. Well, the man called 'Ollie' in the trial fits the description of the man who established this account in the first place. That woman that Mr. Porter had on the stand has a strong connection to Ollie so I thought I would get a hold of you and see what you think about this account because there hasn't been any activity on it for over six months and I don't think there ever will be."

"Are you allowed to tell me how much is in it?"

"Not suppose too, but I'm going to anyway… Over $75,000."

"Gee! That sure would help someone out, wouldn't it?"

"That's why I called you."

"Let me talk to J C Blevins about it. He seems to be protecting Ester Haynes a lot lately."

We smiled at each other and both of us knew I meant that J C was not just protecting Ester Haynes, but certainly enjoyed being around her.

Later that day I tried to contact Blevins but couldn't; I guess he likes being away from the courtroom as much as I do.

I returned to the La Mancha and for some reason walked down to the gazebo which I seldom do during the day. Maybe I am avoiding people I thought. But it was a big mistake on my part for I didn't have time to escape the Reverend Crabtree as I failed to see him until he was half way down the boardwalk.

He paused as he saw me and then looking around to make sure he had an audience, he exclaimed, "You who spread the word of the idiot! Who spreads the nonsense of the heathen! You cretin! You blasphemer who shall be judge by the evil which comes from out of the desert." He pointed and jabbed his cane in the direction of the Air Command property.

But suddenly he did a very strange thing. He just stood quietly and silent for several seconds, shuddered and looked intently to the west, "But… Damn it to Hell… Good shall come from there. Good shall save some of you." What did he say, I thought? He just contradicted everything he has ever said about the Air Command property. It was like he had an epiphany right before my eyes. What does he mean now that 'Good' will come from there? What a piece of crap he is, I think to myself.

Crabtree who is way too young to be 'burned out' of ministering to a church as he claims, says he moved his wife and her relatives to the La Mancha from up in Kentucky where he pastored a Pentecostal church. He looks more like he has done hard physical labor for most of his life instead of being a Man of God as he says he is. He does have that loud piercing voice that so many zealots seem to have.

He's like Josephine Jones was—a mystery. She had paid cash for her condo up on the top floor of the Dolphin building when she had suddenly appeared at the La Mancha about four years ago in late May. Now, here was Crabtree doing the same thing but buying two condos in the Pelican with a suitcase full of dollars. That coincident had not escaped our 'gossip' sessions either.

Bicycle Bob came whizzing down the walk overhearing Crabtree's message and once again save me from this funny little man, "Shut your mouth! Do it now, and get away from here. You are disturbing the guests."

Crabtree looked like a disciplined rude little kid as he hurried back around the Pelican building

20
Redemption is Tough

It all seemed like a bad dream now; he remember the blow by blow slaps as they had struck each while they were sprawled in the broken glasses and the wreck of the table on the floor of her bedroom. He remembered thinking he would really hurt her if he hit her again and he remembered taking her little black box of keys from the bedside table as he left.

He had planned to get on Interstate 10, head east and never come back, but his whole life changed when he had turned around and gone back to Fort Walton Beach making the decision up in Alabama when he was originally running away. That's where he bought the bright red Buick and the five rolling luggage totes, completely changed his appearance by bleaching his hair and purchasing clothes so unlike those he had been accustomed to, and had returned and pulled his courage together to rent a condo at the La Mancha next to the one Joe had owned.

He got even more courage from some source as he went around to the five banks in Destin and Fort Walton Beach with the totes and took the money out of the safety deposit boxes. Launie had given him the right to open the boxes when he turned twenty-one because she was afraid of losing the money somehow and wanted someone to have it at least but the strings she attached were the usual, "I'll cut you clear off if you try to screw me and take it without my permission."

For most of his twenty-eight years, her threats and rules had worked on him and he followed her demand. But her reaction to Joe's death had settled it for him. She didn't care about him or Joe and she had said so. He remembered it like it was last night, "You have to go back out there and find her. You can't let her stay out there. A shipment will be dumped out there in a couple of days and we can't have her found and police boats snooping around." All she was afraid of was getting caught with drugs on her hands.

That's when he had stopped hitting her for he was so damn mad he knew he would seriously hurt her if he hit her again.

Joe had committed the worst possible act trying to please her—gone to Sweden and came back a woman--and that had backfired on him because she still didn't care about him. He felt ashamed that he had avoided Joe after that but he wasn't able to forgive him, his big brother was gone and he didn't like what was left.

After he took the money, he didn't want it for himself at all so he started giving it away. He thought of the trip to the church in Destin and laughed aloud when he thought what might have happened when someone opened the envelope with almost $400,000 in large bills in it. Somehow that person became a little old lady who had counted the offering for years and he imagined her reaction—she would first stare in disbelief and then started shouting like an angel had landed and then faint. He laughed.

Then when Launie's stinking place burned down, he had what he thought was the most ironical idea he ever had, he gave three million of Launie's dollars for a technological school for the young people of Okaloosa County to be built on the land when her strip joint had stood.

Personally for him, his biggest treasure was finding his and Joe's birth certificates in the last bank box he had emptied. He knew for the first time in his life what he real name was—Chuck Kroeger.

He cried the day he finally did leave Fort Walton Beach while visiting Joe's grave at Memorial Cemetery and laughed later when he imagined someone finding the bottle of Dewar's White Label on the tombstone he had erected for Joe's grave. He hoped whoever found it enjoyed it as much as he and Joe used to when they were not old enough to buy it but swiped it from Launie's stock.

Chicago had been good for him as he was on his own for the first time in his life. He felt guilty at first for keeping quite a bit of the money for himself but after he walked the streets of Chicago and saw the many people roaming around looking for food he knew what to do. He opened the Soup Kitchen and now he and his girlfriend, Katie, and the volunteers helping them could not keep up with the lines of people who came to have their one meal of the day.

He felt good about what he was doing and that he had deposited quite a bit of the money in Fort Walton Beach for the Prof to use as he saw fit, but Chuck knew inside that all his good deeds and helping others would not clear his mind of the wrongs he had done by picking up all those packages of drugs as he steered the *Lollipop* through the waves to hook them and take them to Launie. How many people had he harmed, even killed because of that?

It had rained on him nearly all the way from Chicago on his way back to Fort Walton Beach to turn himself in. Between Pensacola and Fort Walton Beach, the rain had stopped and the sun was shining through what remained of the clouds. A magnificent rainbow appeared out on the Gulf as he neared Fort Walton Beach and he took that as a sign he was doing the right thing. He had kissed Katie good-bye and she had asked him to marry her and stay there. He had a funny feeling about her asking instead of him, but had said he would be back.

Highway 98 was just as congested as he remembered even though it was fall already but he finally arrived at the stoplight at Memorial Drive. He turned left and went for several blocks coming to the long line of ancient Eastern Red Cedar trees that someone had planted in a very straight row that marked the boundary of the cemetery as you approach the gate. Those cedars are well over thirty feet tall as their trunks were trimmed bare up at least fifteen feet and the rest of the neatly trimmed trees arose about that and the trunks were as big around as his muscular waist. He turned in at the big ornate gate and started winding around the perimeter of the huge old cemetery. Someone had done some intelligent planning when the cemetery was laid out many years ago and had left large spaces wide enough to create roads; they must have been carriage lanes a one time but now were wide enough for cars to go in both directions on them.

The squares created by the roads had been given names: Prayer, Faith, Good Shepherd, and one that made Chuck laugh—Slumberland. Joe's grave was in the Faith Square. He often felt guilty that he hadn't come forward and taken care of Joe's funeral but he was not strong enough then so he had watched as the Prof and some people at the La Mancha had done a very good job taking care of Joe's last rites. Once he had wondered who paid for the nice casket and the flowers but he realized Joe probably had stacks of money that one of Launie's girls delivered to him each month.

He drove straight to the grave like he had been there last night instead of a year ago, stopped the car but didn't get out but just looked from the car's window. He smiled a sad little smile and after a few minutes drove on. He had to find a place to stay and he had two or three things he really wanted to do before he walked into the police station to surrender or before someone recognized him and he got arrested, and he didn't know if he would get to do them.

21

Red Tide and Anguish-This is Tough, Joe

He rented a room at one of the motel/inn type complexes on Okaloosa Island. He thought about returning to the La Mancha but was afraid that someone there might recognize him. He had grown out his hair again and it wasn't bleached as it had been when he came back to Fort Walton Beach that first time when he cleaned out Launie's safety deposit boxes and left her that note. He once again looked like the Chuck who used to wonder around the Island, eat most of his meals at Tides Inn, and who lived in the nicest penthouse on the Blvd. He was being cautious now about meeting anyone he knew or bumping into anyone who might remember him so he was eating fast food, visiting Joe's grave, and staying in the inn's room.

He felt his will to finish what he had come to do waver and for over two weeks he did nothing to solve things. He visited Memorial Cemetery several times where he sat on the lawn next to Joe's grave but he had seen the same woman there several times and thought he knew her and that she might know him, so he was being particularly careful now when he went there making sure she wasn't there. Katie had told him during several of their phone calls to just come back to Chicago and they would work things out later together. He told her that he was here and that he didn't want her involved in this mess anyway.

Hurricane Patricia, the strongest storm ever recorded over water, hit the western coast of Mexico and dissipated into a tropical depression in a matter of hours as it wore itself out hitting the mountains as it traveled over northern Mexico and so all the meteorologists in Florida were saying that the Panhandle wouldn't feel its effects; that was a few days ago and it had fizzled out except for the heavy downpours that flooded many parts of Texas. The Panhandle of Florida should have been spared any effect of the storm, but due to the lines of squall after squall of rain storms and high winds across the Gulf, disaster had hit the beaches along Okaloosa Island. After three days of heavy rains huge waves took away many beachfronts to where there was very little beach left. The horrid Red Tide, algae that came right after the rains, 'bloomed' and sent its poison into the water and air so the beaches were piled with thousands of dead fish. All the sea birds vanished as they had no use for the poisoned fish. It was a natural occurrence that has disrupted the life along the Gulf coast for centuries.

When Chuck looked out his balcony door one morning, he saw the reddish tint of the water and the dead fish floating to the beach on the waves. He stood in disbelief and opened the door. A fit of coughing and sneezing hit him and his eyes began to water so he quickly shut the balcony door. He wondered how long it would last as he called the front desk. The woman told him that this hadn't happened in seven or eight years and no one could tell how long the algae would stay in close enough to the beach to affect the fish and the humans who breathed the air because no one knew what the currents would do with the algae. He thanked her for the information and went into his bath room to wash his face which didn't seem to help at all. He thought, 'I sure picked a good time to return to get rid of my guilt.'

He decided to get away from the beach and since he wanted to see Joe, he drove down Memorial Drive to the cemetery and entered the gate. He saw the attractive woman with a little boy sitting on the grass playing some sort of game. He thought about leaving but passed by her and drove over by Joe's grave.

He suddenly knew who the woman was, one of Launie's 'dancers,' which he had always tried to have nothing to do with. He detested them and realized he did because they took all of Launie's attention from him and Joe because they made her money. As he turned to look back at her, he saw her quickly pushing the baby's stroller out the gate and up the sidewalk along Memorial Drive.

He got out and sat down on the grass and started talking to the grave, "I don't know what to do. I thought I would just come down here and turn myself in, but it's tough, Joe. I'm going to wait until Sunday and go over to that church in Destin, come back to see you one more time, and then make up my mind if I can do this. Jail doesn't scare me. Oh, I'm not saying I want to be behind bars. I sure wish you were here to talk to about this as we always talked about things together. Being embarrassed by what I have done doesn't worry me either because I am ready for people to know. But being away from Katie who I love and the people who I care about is tough. I know you might not understand for we never knew about redemption and doing what's right for we were never taught, but Joe I need to pray here by your grave. I hope you hear it and much more that He hears and guides me to do what I should do."

If anyone had seen Chuck as he sat crossed-legged on the grass by Joe's grave, they might have thought he was sick with grieve or that he might be hurt. He was there a long time and finally stood up. His eyes were filled with tears as he said again, "This is tough, Joe."

He looked up and a police car was pulling through the front gate of the cemetery. He thought in a flash that here was his chance of making things right but he had those things he wanted to do first. He hurried to his car and drove out a side gate. The police car didn't follow, so he would go to church Sunday and then make his decision.

22

I'm Scared, J C

Blevins knew that Ester took Mitch to Memorial Cemetery often where she sat on a bench along the path that led to Ollie's grave and little Mitch played on the lawn or around Ollie's grave rearranging the beer can medallions that were still there. Mitch was just beginning to stand on his own and take a few steps but he made quick work of collecting the medallions as he crawled over the grave. Ester smiled at him and knew Ollie would approve. Blevins wondered why the old man who took care of the cemetery hadn't thrown the crushed beer cans away and found out that he had but Ester had retrieved them and now the old man left them alone.

As she sat on the bench later one afternoon a red car came in the gate and parked over in another part of the cemetery. A young man got out and walked to a grave, a young man who looked very familiar to Ester. It was the way he walked, she figured out. The man seemed uninterested in her, but she gathered Mitch and his things, loaded him in his stroller and left by a side gate on her way back to Pleasant Street. Every once in a while, she glanced over her shoulder to see if anyone was behind her.

Two days later she sat in the same place before lunch time as it was her day off from the grocery store and the same car came in the gate. This time it slowed down when it went past her and she turned her head away from the man who was driving. He drove on and she saw him park where he was two days earlier and get out of the car. He had some kind of scissors in his hand it appeared. He walked to a grave, sat down on the grass and starting clipping the grass from the base of a tombstone. He returned to the car a little later and came back to the grave carrying a brown paper bag she recognized as a 'bottle bag.' He pulled out a bottle of something from it, took several big gulps from the bottle and then poured the rest onto the grave. She thought he glanced her way as he returned to the car and drove away.

Toward the end of the week, it happened again. This time she was sitting on the ground with her back against a tree playing with Mitch. She loved little Mitch so much as he was becoming a 'real' person. He was a robust eater and had developed pudgy fat cheeks that were continuously curved upward in a happy smile. His favorite new thing was to sit and listen to her read to him and when she brought out the old ragged book that Ollie had kept since Old Mitch had given it to him in Congo Park in New Orleans when he was a kid of thirteen, Little Mitch had grabbed it in his little hands and started chewing on the hard cover. Ester knew he must be getting a tooth and she let him chew the old book to his heart's content. It was the most prized possession she had that had belonged to Ollie and now it was Little Mitch's--the real prized possession that Ollie had given her.

The red car pulled into the cemetery and slowly went past where they were and traveled on over to park in its usual place. The man got out of the car, walked to the grave and sat down on the grass. Ester watched him closely and thought he shoulders were shaking like he might be crying and then she heard him say, "Okay, I'll do it."

She was really frightened and immediately left the cemetery pushing Mitch as fast as she could. She thought there could be people around that were mad at her for her testimony in court and she was afraid for Mitch and herself. She called J C and told him what had been going on. He was all the way over in Crestview taking food to those two kids who had seen Ollie's murder. He promised he would come by later that evening. "I'm really scared, J C. I think I know that man."

23

Sam Ripley and Alice Pearl

Sam Ripley and his fiancée Alice Pearl held each other tight many nights after that horrible night they were on a sand dune overlooking where the Black Drainage Ditch empties into the Sound about two miles west of Fort Walton Beach. They had gone to the high bank where they could look all the way across the Sound to where the waves of the Gulf hit Okaloosa Island and now there was no way in the world that Sam could have taken Alice back to that place; that place where they had spent many happy times spread out on a blanket, watching the star filled sky, and making plans for their future.

Sam is a Med Corpsman at Eglin and Alice works in one of the banks in Fort Walton Beach. She had followed Sam from Branson, Missouri where they both grew up to Fort Walton Beach so they could be close together. Every minute Sam could be off the base, the two of them were doing something together; paddle boarding on the Choctawhatchee Bay, snorkeling in the Gulf, or lying in their favorite spot enjoying a picnic and bottle of wine and going to 'second base,' as both of them had sworn to save themselves till their upcoming marriage next January.

But that fateful night when Launie steered her big blue yacht, the *Lollipop*, up against the shore where a huge pond had been dredged to create the channel for the many barges that travel down the Sound, they lay there and watch in horror at what happened after Launie gave Ollie the *More Fun Comic* that introduces Oliver Queen as the Green Arrow. They saw Ollie turn into a little boy getting his very best present at Christmas. Then they saw her take the little gold plated revolver from her pocket as Ollie sat with his back to her at the little table at the rear of the yacht getting ready to open the plastic cover to take out his treasure. Launie barely flinch as she shot him in the back of his neck. They saw the happiness on his face as it seemed to crumble into shock as the bullet hit his head and a look of seeing eternity crossed his face.

Alice screamed as she saw what was going to happen but Launie had shot the gun at the exact same time and did not hear Alice. Sam held his hand over Alice's mouth as Launie handcuffed Ollie to the buckets of paint sitting on the back loading ramp of the yacht and struggle to push them and Ollie over the back edge into the forty feet of water. They saw her throw the little gun in after him.

As the yacht was pulling away, Sam held the hysterical Alice in one arm as he punched in the numbers his cell phone calling the military police on Eglin who quickly alerted the Sheriff's office at Fort Walton Beach. Launie was arrested as she walked up the gravel path from the little dock back of the Dorm where Ollie and the girls lived.

Now months later, J C Blevins had told them they would testify in court two days from now. Blevins had provided them with several different places to live since the murder as they lived in fear around the clock. This late afternoon they were in a cute little apartment in Crestview. They had moved seven or eight times in the last year and Sam had asked for and gotten leave from the Air Force so he could be with Alice.

From outside somewhere they heard a crash and then a woman hollering. All at once there was a frantic knock on their door and a woman was shouting and crying to be let in. Before Sam could stop her, Alice was sliding the chain off the lock and as he stepped beside her to slam the door, it jerked open knocking Alice into him.

Three figures all with black stocking caps pulled down over their faces with holes in them so they could see burst into the room. One of them took charge and got right in Sam's face, "Listen, you dumb shit, you do as I say or we are going to hurt your woman. Understand?" Seeing the revolver she had pointed straight at Alice, Sam just shook his head.

Minutes later Sam and Alice with duct tape over their mouths and rolled into blankets were dumped into the bed of an old pick-up. For several miles, Sam could feel that the pavement was smooth and once he thought they must be out on the Interstate because they were traveling so fast, but suddenly the pick-up made almost a right angle turn and it went bumping down a dark road which actually looked like a path to Sam as he got a glimpses of it through a hole in the floor of the pick-up. He knew he had to keep his head about him because Alice was huddled against his back and he could hear and feel her sobbing.

The pick-up stopped and the tailgate was jerked open. The two of them were tossed onto the ground. Sam could feel the hands go under his waist and saw that he was being lifted off the ground. She threw him over her shoulder in a fireman's carry as Sam realized they were all women. Over to his right, he saw another of them pick up Alice in the same way. For a second he felt some pride as he saw she was struggling frantically to free herself.

Fifty feet of so in front of them was a decrepit old building which Sam would discover was a tool shed. He felt himself flying over the shoulder of the woman carrying him and was stunned from the landing on the hard dirt floor of the building. Suddenly, Alice came crashing down on top of him. He felt his shoes being removed and that he was rolling over and over on the floor. He rolled out of the blanket and felt two hands undoing his pants. He struggled to keep them on but could feel them being pulled off over his feet.

The obvious leader of the three pulled plastic ties from her hip pocket and while she held her gun to Alice's head Sam felt the plastic pull tight and watched as they did the same to Alice. The leader bent over and almost hissed in his ear, "Listen you dumb prick, if you make any move toward the door as we leave, I will shoot your pecker and the boys off. You hear me?" The other two stood at the door ready to leave but the one in charge kicked Sam in the head. Through the pain, he heard a chain being drug through the latches on the outside of the door and heard the lock snap shut between two links in the chain.

It didn't take Alice long to saw the plastic tie off her wrists on a rusty nail she found on the wall. A few seconds later Sam was free also but they soon discovered that there were no windows in the little building and that the door was solid and they could not bust through it.

The two of them stood huddled together and tried to console each other. Sam realized Alice also only had her underwear on and he was embarrassed that he was suddenly aroused. Alice was crying on his shoulder as he tried to erase his thoughts and talk to her, "We'll make it. I promise. We will get out of here somehow."

"We're out in the woods somewhere. I could tell as we bumped along that dirt path," Alice almost shouted.

"I know. I tried to keep thinking along the way with every turn we made. We were on Interstate 10 I think, and then we turned right so that had to be north and if must have been thirty minutes from there before we turned onto that path. I think we are up in the Black Water State Park somewhere."

"No one comes up here this late in the year. We may be here until…."

"Stop it! We are going to get out of this. I promise."

24

Sunday Afternoon Visitors

Somehow he didn't have trouble finding Faith Lutheran in Destin today like he had last year when he decided to visit and give the big Treasury Notes and large denomination bills to the church. He hope the little pastor with the goatee was there and as things happened, Pastor Greg was there and was delivering the message.

Chuck had the *Bible* he had unintentionally taken with him that Sunday last year when he was trying to escape after the service without going through a line of people who were stopping to talk with the pastor. It was one of the reasons he needed to be here this morning—to return it to the holder in a pew. He smiled as he remember last year he didn't know where *Hebrews* was in the *Bible* but could quickly turn to *John 2:17* which was the passage for the sermon today. He was sure no one would remember him for last year he had his hair bleached very blonde and was wearing a awful leisure suit and besides that the church had been full of tourists. He felt relax today as he recognized what the service was all about and how it proceeded from one point to another. He almost uttered a sound as the scripture was read for he knew without a doubt it was directed straight to him. It was what he needed to hear so he would have courage to finish what he had come back to do. He shook Pastor Greg's hand as he left and thanked him. Pastor Greg said he was glad Chuck was there and wished him a good week ahead and hoped he would come back.

He drove back to Fort Walton Beach and thought about turning right on Santa Rosa Blvd to go see the new tech center the city was building with the money he had sent, but he thought it would just bring back memories that would make him angry for Launie's place had stood where it was being built, so he turned left like he was going to his Inn Suites but passed it and continued on down the Blvd. He glanced up at the condo he used to live in and thought about the expensive clothes he had left there because he was afraid of being caught if he went back for them. He laughed to himself as he thought he sure wasn't wearing that kind of clothes now and then he laughed out loud as he thought he certainly was happier now. He made the left turn off the Blvd and pulled up to the gate at the La Mancha.

I was sitting on my balcony with my binoculars watching a pod of dolphins fishing out away from our beach. They were all adults or almost adults for it was late in the season and the babies had grown big during the summer. The Red Tide had left us almost as quickly as it had appeared. We were very thankful that it had been pulled back out into the Gulf after invading our beaches for only two days and three nights. Everyone in Okaloosa County knew the stretch of water in front of the La Mancha and on west was good fishing waters and the dolphins certainly did; they were the best indication that the water was once again safe for the fish and safe for our visitors and us.

I saw Jonathan L dive into shallowed water and come up with some kind of little fish and fly back to his perch on the volleyball goal post so the gulls were fishing again also. During the Red Tide I had not seen a gull on our beach or in the air around our beach. Peter Sellers remark of 'Swine Bird' still enters my mind occasionally especially when Jonathan or a relative of his tries to poop on me but they are a lot smarter than most people believe..

I was lucky as I sat there as I saw the Air Patrol flying toward me— those magnificent in flight Brown pelicans. There must be an air current that pulls them in and lets them swoop over the pool between the Dolphin and the Pelican buildings for they do it almost every day. As I watched as least thirty of them glided by, and the leader of the V shaped formation diverted from what I thought their pattern was going to be and swerved out over the gazebo and almost straight out from the La Mancha over the Gulf as all the others followed. They, too, were fishing and way out from the shore which pleased me much.

My cell phone rang and Gerald said someone wanted to come up and see me. I asked who and he said the man knew me and knew where I lived, so I agreed and said send him on.

I answered the knock on my door and opened it to who I thought at first was a total stranger. He held out his hand and said, "I'm Chuck Kroeger. You probably remember me as Chuck Jenkins for that is what they called me then."

I was surprised but shook hands with him and ask, "What can I do for you?"

"I would like to talk with you for a while, if you have time."

"Sure. Sure. Come in." I looked down in a parking space in front of the Pelican and saw the bright red car. All the postcards I had received popped into my mind for they all had a picture of that same car. "Let's go out and sit on the balcony," I said as I walked toward the sliding screen as the weather was so nice that I had the door open, "I never thought I would see you here in Fort Walton Beach again."

"I didn't expect to come back either but I have decided to try to straighten things out that I was a part of—things that hurt a lot of people."

As I sat down on one of the tall bar stools, I said, "Redemption is a good thing, but doing good things don't seem to count unless you've changed inside."

"I'm not sure how I was inside. No one ever ask me what I thought. I just did what Launie Sanderson told me to do. Young minds are gullible and sometimes they mind their elders," he said as he too sat down.

"Yes, I've found that to be true. You might not know it, but I taught school before I retired down here."

"Oh, I know that. I know quite a bit about you Prof or I wouldn't have bothered you with that money you found in that account."

"And I knew it was you who was sending it too. Why did Launie Sanderson have such a big influence on you?"

"She was the only adult that my brother Joe and I had in our family but she wasn't there much for us. We had to fend for ourselves and hang together. That's why we felt so hopeless."

"You had a brother Joe?" Suddenly I realize who she was, "My lands, Josephine Jones was your brother? Would you like a bottle of water as we sit and talk, because I need one?"

"That would be great as my throat is really dry as it always is when I think about these things. Yes, Joe did what I thought unconceivable to himself thinking he was pleasing Launie. By the way, I know what you did for him for I, too, was at the funeral that day even though none you saw me and I know that you have his dog. I want to thank you for that too."

"Thank you, but there wasn't anyone around to do it," I said as I walked in to the kitchen and came back with two bottles of water.

"I know." There was a long pause, "You need to know also that Launie is my, our, mother."

We were sitting on the balcony and he had said that as I took a swig of water and I nearly spit it out as his last statement nearly floored me, "You are serious, aren't you?"

"Yes."

"Well, I can see where you would have no guidance from her and might do the crazy things she had you do. I think others will also."

"I want you to call that DEA agent who was here last summer— you know, the big black man who finally caught Launie."

"I think Marvin would disagree with you about catching her. He told me that she probably could have escaped if she hadn't shot Ollie."

"And that's another thing, Ollie was one of the best guys I have ever known. He never hurt anyone. People thought he was retarded or something, but he wasn't. He just wanted to be alone and to create his own world. I can sure understand that. Nobody will ever know what that guy went through as a kid and teenager."

I looked at him and thought 'like you and Joe did?' but I said, "I'll try to call Marvin for you. You want me to do it now?"

"If you will…."

Marvin was amazed when I told him who was on my balcony with me and told me he would over as quickly as he could.

Thirty minutes later Marvin knocked on my door and as I introduced him to Chuck, he said, "I followed you like a blood hound for months and had many chances to bring you in but my real goal was to get Launie Sanderson and see her behind bars so I left you alone."

"I knew you too. I was living the last few months before I ran away in total fear of opening my door or seeing you pull up beside the *Lollipop* and arresting me."

"The Prof told me something when they reassigned me last fall. Remember, Prof? Something like Shakespeare would write I guess.

"Maybe but you tell us for I told you many things. Which thing was it?"

"Ha. You going to make me sound like Billy Shakespeare? Well, he said that in the worst tragedies ever written or lived, innocent people have been caught up in the scheme of things and sometimes those innocent ones become heroes if they can escape."

"That's not all that was said."

Marvin looked out over the Gulf we could see so clearly from where we were sitting, "I said, I hope he getting a peacefulness and joy from doing what he's doing. And that's why we need you Marvin. Yeah, I want to use you, my friend."

"What for?"

"Chuck wants to give himself up and turn himself in to J C Blevins and I want you to go with him."

Marvin didn't hesitate, "Sure I'll do that and I'll stand with him in any court." He turned to Chuck, "I know what happened to you and why you were doing what you did."

Chuck smiled for the first time since he had come into my condo. He stood up and stepped over and stretch out his hand across the little bar table to Marvin. Marvin's big broad hand almost enclosed his as they shook hands.

"Now, there is another thing we could do," Marvin said.

"What?"

"Let's call both J C Blevins and Prosecuting Attorney Curtis Porter and see what they are doing."

I grasped what he had in mind and said, "Sure, why not?"

Sometimes things just go right and the best laid plans of mice and men do work out as an hour later, Porter and Blevins sat on the balcony with us. We were crowded together and sitting so close we had to look each other in the eyes. Chuck told Porter who he was and what he had done and that he was ready to take whatever came his way. Porter listened with more intentness than I had seen in the courtroom even. He took out a note pad and scribbled something every once in a while.

When Chuck stopped, Porter said, "How about giving up your rights to a jury trial and let me appoint a judge—or retired judge to hear your case? You can have a bench trial and I have a couple of grad students from the University of Florida Law School who can help you with the procedures if you want?"

Chuck looked at me and then at Marvin, and when Marvin shook his head yes, Chuck said, "Yes, sir, I will agree for I think you are a fair and honest man because these two here do."

"And now we need to get Judge Bickel in on this for he is the presiding judge of Okaloosa County and he has to agree," Porter said. "I know where he is right now because I passed the Yacht Club on the way here and saw his car. Let's just see what he's up to."

Porter called the judge's number and I heard him explain what was happening and where we all were. He disconnected the call on his cell and said, "He wants to come out here now. That sure is a surprise. He's on his way."

I called Gerald at the security house and told him I was having more company.

In just a few minutes, Bickel knocked on my door and I let him in. I led him to my balcony which was now very full and I thought I saw a look of contempt cross his face as Marvin introduced him to Chuck but he leaned across the table and shook hands with Chuck much like Marvin had earlier.

It didn't take Porter very long to tell Bickel what the plans were, and Bickel readily agreed.

"We will need some security for Judge Boyd's little court if she agrees to hear the case. How about loaning her that young woman who is helping in your court?" Porter asked.

"I agree that you will need someone but I don't want to disrupt things in Launie Sanderson's trial any more than they already are," Bickel said as he turned to J C Blevins, "Can't you find someone to help Judge Boyd?"

"We'll find someone," Blevins answered.

I was sitting thinking and looking out across the way while this conversation was happening and I saw Bob coming around the end of the Dolphin building on his bike. I glanced at my cell phone to see the time and realized we had been here a long time. Bob circled the pool house and was coming down the walk right beneath my balcony and we heard the familiar 'oooga' 'oooga' of his bicycle horn. I saw him glance up and take a double take as he waved up toward me as he always does. Oh good Lord, I thought, I hope he doesn't just come on up here. He didn't as he swerved and went down the walk at the end of my building and sped away.

Everyone agreed on the plan and Porter said he had to convince Judge Boyd. Everyone left and I sat down again as the sun was sitting behind a huge almost black cloud.

Blevins took Chuck to the jail across the Sound and put him in a single cell up on the third floor away from all the other prisoners. I agreed that the red Buick could remain where it was in front of my building and that I would say it belonged to my company; it sat there until Chuck's trial

114

was over. Blevins thought about talking to Chuck about all his visits to the cemetery as he took him to jail but decided that could wait.

All of us knew that Chuck would be in danger once certain people discovered he had returned. I laughed later when I remembered that the third floor was for women and that Launie had been kept up there also.

25

Convincing a Judge

For some inane reason, Judge Bickel had announced there would be no court session again today. I wondered how long the people of the community would put up with the trial and how long the jury would stand still for being sequestered from their families and friends because Bickel had decided last week that they would be staying together at one of the hotels in the area—one that was a secret from the public, he and they thought.

I was watching some sandpipers as they would suddenly scamper across the sand, stop and peck frantically, and then run again with their quick little steps. I was sitting on the perimeter wall in front of those two sea oats I had planted there and Paul Bishop laughed his way into my mind. Paul was seldom far from my mind these days as the horrific happenings of this summer reminded me so much of the ones that happened last summer. Paul's life reminded me a little of what Chuck went through; the love Paul had in his life didn't stop him from having tragic things happen to him ending in his untimely death with his girlfriend out on Highway 98 just as the hate and abuse hadn't stopped Chuck from escaping into a life he now loved. They were opposites but the two opposing ends wrapped around and created a circle in my mind.

My cell phone rang and it was Porter who asked if I could meet him at the jail and go with him to talk with Chuck. I was surprised he would want me with him but he told me Chuck surely trusted me for I was the one he had approached to start solving his problems, so I told Porter certainly and that I was on my way.

We took the elevator to the third floor and were soon seated in a little conference room. Porter said, "Chuck, I want you to read an article from the *NorthWest Daily* and then we can talk. It's somewhat long, but I want you to really get what's being said in it for I believe it is very true about Judge Boyd." He pulled the article from his briefcase and I saw it was something I had already read and had saved for I wanted to meet this woman.

From *Who We Should Know*

Judge Bonita Boyd

She came into the world in 1939 in a traditional Hogan built by her grandmother's family in the depths of Canyon de Chelly by a fast running creek near the Four Corners area of the West. Her grandmother was chosen to name her and the first word out of the old woman's wrinkled sun bronzed mouth was 'bonita." The old woman was wise for she was a terribly beautiful baby.

She arrived in this world just as the sun peeked over the top of Eastern Holy Mountain so holding her in one arm and gathering a handful of maize in the other her mother had stood in the doorway, scattered the maize on the ground, and held Bonita up toward the bright sun—her eyes glistened but she didn't blink.

Chuck stopped and looked at Porter, but Porter said, "Go on, you'll understand in a minute, I think."

Her father had performed the 'Blessing Way' that night as all the family sat on the dirt floor of the Hogan and sang the blessing. Later, she learned all the words as did her brothers and sisters: 'This home, my home, shall be surrounded with *sa'ah naaghei bikk'eh hazhoo.* May I live in this home happily and peacefully and with respect. May my house be in harmony: From my head, may I be happy, To my feet, may I be happy, All around me, may I be happy, May my fire be well made and happy, May the sun my mother's ancestor, be happy from this gift, May I be happy as I walk around my house, May this road of light, my mother's ancestor, be happy.'

Chuck started to stop again but this time I said, "Go on. You'll want to meet this woman."

She had learned it well for it was not her house that she thought about when she sang the blessing, but herself, and she had accomplished nearly all the happy blessings.

She was the prettiest of all the little girls in elementary and middle school in Chinle, Arizona but no one was ever jealous of her because of her grace and good manners. In high school, she succeeded in everything she attempted from cross country running to the hardest classes at the little school.

She graduated from Arizona State and was persuaded to enter the Miss Navajo Nation pageant which she did thinking she could use the money if she won any. She did as she won the pageant and immediately enter law school at the University of New Mexico Law School where she quickly became a favorite among her fellow students because of her quiet humor, good manners, and helpful attitude.

She chose to move to Florida to become an advocate for the Seminoles as they struggled to hold on to their traditions and land with the ever increasing intrusions around them. She defended them well and gained recognition by the Governor who appointed her to the State Court of Appeals and ten years later, she was the Senior Judge of that court.

She outlived her husband of many years, Charles Boyd, who was also a lawyer and judge. Their six children blessed her with many grandchildren. When she retired in 2011, she moved into a little bungalow which faces east on the Sound in Mary Ester a few miles west of Fort Walton Beach. She lives there with her Australian Sheep dog, Coxy.

When Chuck stopped this time, he said, "Oh, I think I know where you are going now. You want Judge Boyd to hear my case?"

"Yes, if I can convince her to," Porter said. "I have convinced her to come down here today and she is waiting in the next room. Would you like to meet her?"

Chuck frowned as he thought he had been sit up maybe, looked at me and I just smiled, and the he said "Yes, sir. Sounds like she is almost too good to be true and I'm sure she will be fair."

"Legally, she probable shouldn't see you until you stand before her as a defendant, but Judge Bickel has agreed and I certainly have so I'll go ask her to come in here."

When Porter had gone, I looked at Chuck and said, "I don't know how things could go better for you. Oh, I don't think you are home free, but I think you will get an honest square deal."

When Porter and Judge Boyd came back, Chuck and Judge Boyd met for the first time. She looked him steadily in the face getting up close so she could see his eyes, "Young man, I don't know you yet, but I will and then I will be fair with you. Now, you have some homework for me. I want you to write everything you can think of that has happened in your life. Don't be a silly high school boy and write a few sentences. You have all the time in the world because you are going to stay right here in this cell until you finish if you expect me to hear your case."

She turned to Porter and said, "And we will need some help with this and an armed guard to stand outside the room as we progress through this."

Porter replied, "I'm ahead of you for once, Judge Boyd, as I've already told Chuck about two grad students who are working for me this semester. You can have them at your disposal as long as you need them.

One of them will interest you very much, I think. Oh, I don't put down the other one, but the young woman is from Albuquerque and I think you night just hit it off with her."

"Good Lord, what is she doing in Florida? Judge Boyd asked.

"I guess she might ask you the same thing, so it might have something to do with you as I heard her talking about you to the young man who is the other one I will loan you."

"Sounds good to me. We'll get whatever is bothering Chuck taken care of and let him get on with his life."

I smiled, Porter smiled, and Chuck simply nodded his head yes.

26

Someone knows too much

Our group avoids Crabtree and we have moved most of our discussions to when we are eating with each other in one of our condos. Our biggest question besides who Crabtree really is, is who are the women?

Walkin Al says he thinks he has seen one of them before. We all laughed and teased him when he said that just like we laughed at him that day at the big Y pool that day in June when he got a call from one of his 'women.'

Al Dollars is retired United States Air Force, a Lieutenant Colonel, who has travel the world and still does. He has many women in his list of contacts who admire him and are happy to accompany him whenever he goes on a trip.

We had been talking about the first body that washed up on our beach that June, nude and with her arms cut off just below the elbows. Gladis said, "And to think that we still didn't know who she was until here a year later when Ester Haynes the same as told us in her testimony. But when that second one washed in, we all saw that it was Josephine Jones but as far as I know no one knows how it happened."

"I remember most when that lunatic went up and down Santa Rosa Blvd shooting arrows at everybody and anything," Bob butted in and then quickly looked at me.

"I remember that too," I said. "But, I remember what happened later most," I rubbed the scars when the arrow had gone clear through my right wrist."

Everyone was quiet for a long time. Gladis broke the silence, "Yes, but you have Skipper now as a result of Josephine's death, even though he has that lop-sided appearance where that other arrow took off part of his ear."

Bob broke in as he often does, "You know, I've lived at the La Mancha two or three times as long as any of you and I've lived in Fort Walton Beach all my life, but I've never seen or heard of anything like what happened here." He looked at me and that broad outrageous smile broke across his wide face, "I'll bet you are getting a good laugh out if it, Prof! A good laugh because it's still all a mystery."

"Well, you're wrong. I'm just as concerned and mystified as all of you seem to be about the whole mess."

"If J C Blevins hadn't been around, we might never have learned what we do know," Walkin Al said. "And, of course, Marvin knew much more the whole time that we ever imagined. Anyone seen or heard from Marvin?"

"He came by to say good-bye to me after Launie was arrested for Ollie's murder and I saw him across the courtroom one day at the trial but didn't get to talk to him," I said. "But, there was something much bigger that Marvin knew about and that I learned a little about. He was in court that day, but like I said, I haven't had a chance to talk to him about what he was doing, and Judge Bickel has made it very clear indeed that this trial is about Ollie's death and nothing else. I guess if Launie is found guilty of Ollie's murder she will go to prison for life and there might not be another trial."

Once again, Bob butted in, "You mean about Launie's drug business? It's a mystery to me how that was all kept so quiet. Something that big should have filled the paper. I always thought it was strange that so many Johns from so many states were visiting that strip joint of hers. I bet I have seen license plates from thirty different states there at different times."

Gladis looked at him, and laughed, "Just what were you doing driving around Launie's place, Bob?"

Bob's big bald head turned a bright pink, "I haven't totally lost interest in women, you know."

"Oh, you've got a competitor, Al," Gladis laughed loudly.

"But, we have been right about one thing, I said. This long drug out trial should have ended a week after it started. J C Blevins found the comic book with Ollie's blood on the plastic jacket right there on the table on the *Lollipop*. Sam Ripley and Alice Pearl saw the whole thing as they hid in the darkness up on that bank above where Launie anchored the *Lollipop*. They saw her shoot Ollie in the back of the head as he was totally engrossed in that comic about his hero, the Green Arrow. They saw Launie handcuff Ollie to those four gallon buckets of paint. And God Almighty, it was sea foam green paint at that. Then they saw her drag and push everything off the end of the yacht into that pond which was just dredged out of the bottom of the Sound."

Suddenly, all of us froze. Our faces came alive after what seemed a full minute and we were all talking at once.

"We're a bunch of dumbasses, Bob blurted out. It was Ollie who shot all those arrows. Why would that comic mean so much to him if he wasn't the jerk who shot up the whole Blvd and you, Prof?"

"And I'm the dumbest of all," I said. "I should have caught it when Ester let it slip out in court."

Al broke in, "It's got to be the answer. Launie kept Ollie hidden up at her joint. Few of the locals had ever seen him. What do you think he was doing all that time back behind that screen in her place when he wasn't being the bouncer?"

A thought enter my head but quickly disappeared as Gladis said, "Well, we will never know just what he had in that little addition to the Dorm where he lived…because of the fire."

"Yeah, that's another strange thing. Launie's place and that other building we called the Dorm burned down to the ground before Ollie was even buried over in Memorial Cemetery. I think someone was snooping around and watching everything and burned the evidence before J C Blevins and his crew could investigate."

"Blevins did go through the place," I said. Remember the paper said he found the place clean and orderly except for Launie's bedroom that had broken whiskey glasses and a bottle of booze all over the floor. That, and the headboard on her big purple bed had been torn apart and the safe hidden inside was standing open and empty. But you are right someone was watching the whole thing as it played out and tried to interrupt the investigation when the buildings were set on fire."

We were all quiet again until Al said, "What do you think Ollie was doing that day when he went down the beach with the metal detector?"

"How did you know about that?" I ask.

"Max finally talked to me one day before Daniel Sheraton fired him from Sun Setter Beach Services. Yeah, I know Max wasn't worth his spit, but Max was just too damn proud for his own good. I mean, he was just a twenty-three-old horny guy who loved to sniff around every woman he saw."

We all laughed and it was Al's turn to turn red.

"Well, all I know is that if it was Ollie when he ran up across the beach and the ramp up to the lawn right in front of my condo in Dolphin, he was carrying something. When Skipper growled and barked at him, he let out a stream of cussing and ran on across the parking lot and out to the Blvd."

"It was drugs!" Bob declared.

"Well, I don't know that either, and you and I both know that Judge Bickel made it very clear that this trial is about Ollie's death and nothing else. Remember, he said he would call a mistrial if Porter or Schaberg said anything about anything other than Ollie's murder?"

"Yeah, I know. I've been sitting right there beside you and I've heard almost everything you have. I don't think we need to worry about Schaberg saying anything else. That shyster is a slick greasy little geek from Miami or I'm truly Humpty Dumpty whenever I ride my bike around the place."

We all laughed at that and since it was well past midnight, we all said thanks to Gladis for having us at her condo and I headed back to Dolphin.

Someone disappeared around the corner in a big hurry as I walked out her patio door. I didn't see who it was, but I'm very sure whoever it was, he or she was listening at the patio door trying to hear our conversation.

You know how it is when you surprise someone and they try to get away without you seeing them. Whoever it was did just that.

27

Early Rendezvous

People who don't live near the ocean often pooh-pooh the idea of a riptide because it is difficult understand how a 'river' can form in the middle of the sea. The idea of currents flowing around the earth deep down in the oceans is common knowledge, but a stream of water forming and going against the rest of the water in the Gulf on the surface is unique and difficult to understand.

This foggy morning, we have a strong riptide pulling away from the beach to places unknown until it finally peters out. It is so strong that if you sit still and look at the surface of the Gulf you can actually see water moving in the opposite direction of the oncoming waves just like a river inside of another body of water.

*

She called him very early this morning. They had met at the gazebo several times and had nearly been 'caught' by the Prof on two or three occasions but Al didn't really care. She was an attractive and interesting woman. After he had admired her body, the long muscular legs and easy to look at bosom, he had discovered that she was actually pretty smart so they did have things to talk about. Sometimes though, he felt she had memorized things she knew he had been involved with when he worked for NASA.

The Prof could tease him all he wanted as their group sat around the pool or in the gazebo enjoying the sitting sun but he intended on meeting her whenever he could. She had given him all her attention and she was a young vibrant good looking woman and he smiled to himself as he realized that was what he lived for.

He had flowers ready to take to her this morning but wondered why she had called so early. She said so they could be together longer before anyone else got up and around—especially the Prof.

He picked up the bouquet of autumn flowers and sat out from the Sea Shell to walk to the gazebo in the misty cool fall air. The fog this morning as it is many fall mornings was so thick he could see only a few yards ahead as he walked down the sidewalk. It crossed his mind that they could just as well meet elsewhere and not have to worry being seen, but he didn't care this morning as he cross the parking lot and walked down the sidewalk by the big pool.

Al Dollar's weakness was women and he knew it. With his training and his many important positions with the Country's space programs he knew he should know better than fall for every woman who had good legs and gave her whole attention to him, but he couldn't resist her nor control himself.

He saw her sitting in the shadows of the gazebo and greeted her in a low quiet voice, "Good Morning, Eva. It is so good to see you this morning."

She had insisted that their conversations be quiet as to not wake up anyone. She had a thermos of hot coffee and some fresh biscuits she had just taken out of the oven.

She walked up very close to Al as she flirted and rubbed against him. Somehow the cheap perfume, and he knew it was cheap, aroused his desire to hold her.

As he reached for her, she said as she poured his coffee, "Oh, let's take our coffee and biscuits down by the water and go wading. Oh, I know it's cold this morning but the water will certainly wake us up!'

127

He was all too eager to go with her and their shoes were off by the time they were at the bottom of the ramp.

They stood in the cold water which touched every nerve in his legs as he shivered. He reached for her with his empty hand, she giggled a teasing little laugh and said, "Wait, I have another surprise for you. I'll run and get it."

When the third or fourth mouth full of the hot coffee hit his stomach Al knew something was wrong. All his training with the Air Force had taught him to take care of himself and now he had let this woman take control of him.

His vision was blurry and his legs would not hold him up much longer he sensed. He slid to the ground and caught himself with his hands. But the crawling position didn't last any longer than the standing one and he quickly was lying flat on his stomach with his face brushing against the cold sand for he couldn't hold his head up.

Water was sloshing up around his head and into his mouth as he felt his body being pulled outward with every wave. Though he could only half see through his nearly closed eyes, he saw two figures coming toward him. He smelled Eva and knew it was her, but the other one was just a blur to him.

Eva with a heavy leather glove on her hand, reached into a cooler and pulled the twisting and slashing snake from it and it tried to coil so it could strike and Al heard a rattling sound. She walked deliberately toward him talking as she came. He thought he heard, "You know too much for you own good, you horny old fart." He watched her as if she were in slow motion and then it was like it was moving one frame of film at a time. She stood over him and the monstrous diamondback lunged at him and the last thing he saw before he blinked was its unblinking serpent eyes. Its wide hideous jaws opened and he felt its needle like fangs sink into the soft skin of his throat.

He wanted to scream and maybe he did but he did not hear a scream. He did feel the venom as it shot into his neck close to the jugular vein. Then everything was slow motion in his mind as his body closed down.

He heard a new voice from up on the gazebo, one that he thought he knew, "You stupid Sons of Bitches, why hell did you kill him? He didn't know anything. You stupid bitch."

Al's body dislodged from the bank as the riptide caught it. The second figure that he had seen as he died had put a stringer of dead fish around his neck. If the animals of the Gulf didn't eat his body, it still might take days, even weeks, for the body to free itself from the riptide and come back into shore somewhere.

Rattlesnakes don't like salt water at all and it turned loose and swam back to the beach, slithering across the sand chased by Eva with her forked snake-catcher.

They zigzagged across the beach but it escaped into a broken place in the beach equipment box. Eva grabbed it and tried to pull it out but the snake was too strong. Its thick six foot long body disappeared into the box. She was left holding the rattles in her hand as they had broken off.

The person that had shouted "Stupid Sons of Bitches' ordered Eva to pick up one of the paddle boards that leaned against the equipment box and carry it across the La Mancha's property to the house over on Tarpon Street. "Hurry up! We've got to get away from here before we get caught down here. If anyone sees your stupid ass, maybe they will just think you are some damn tourist out on the water in this fog. You crazy bitch! Get your ass going."

She picked up Al's shoes from the sand as she went.

I was up and making coffee when I heard the noises coming from below. Taking time to fill my cup, I slide the door open and stepped out into a curtain of fog. And though my eyes were wide open, they might just as well been closed. We have fog frequently during the fall but this morning's enveloped the whole scene below me. Once in a while a little space would break and I could get a glimpse of the ground below and during a little break, I thought I saw a long board passed by and laughed out loud as I thought what in this world would someone be out with a long board in this fog? Whoever was carrying it was on the other side of it as I looked so I thought some silly tourist must be out of their mind. Then I heard a familiar sound as it passed by on the sidewalk that runs along the end of the Pelican but it was distorted and I laughed again.

28

A Few Minutes Later

I stood by the railing of my balcony trying to see through the soupy mess below but got no real picture in my mind about what was happening. Suddenly from the opposite direction to my right, I heard voices again but these were different and in my mind I saw the young couple who come to the La Mancha each year about this time. They have two little girls and the oldest one was the one who announce that the cat would be called 'Poseidon.' They live somewhere up in Illinois and during the last few summers I have enjoyed their visits with their two happy little girls, but now there seemed to be an argument.

"Get your drunk rear end out of here right now. I don't want you waking the girls."

He made his way through the sliding glass doorway she slid open and as he stepped off the concrete porch of the condo onto the lawn, he misgauged the distance and fell face first onto the grass landing on his hands and knees. Cussing loud enough to wake up both buildings, he heard the door almost slam as she shut it after him. He got to his feet and made his way down the sidewalk west of the big Y pool and stumbled down the west boardwalk.

I heard him for I would be surprised if he hadn't roused a lot of people but decided it was none of my business, so I went back in my condo to fix some breakfast.

He laughed loudly and then holding a finger to his mouth, he whispered, "Ssssh! You're so in Time Out young man! Three days at least." He thought that was so funny as he giggled like one of his little girls.

Carefully descending the steps there with great exaggeration, he stopped to hold onto the railing as he carefully put his foot down on the sand from the bottom step. He made big swiping sweeps with his arms to wipe the fog away. He laughed out loud and almost shouted, "That'll show you I'm not stinking drunk like you said."

He didn't know why they had come to the La Mancha this late in the year anyway. They usually came down from Illinois in late June or July—he certainly remembered last year when they were here and all kinds of shit had hit the place.

No one knew about it he thought, but he had been quick enough and brave enough to rush over and look at that first body that had washed up that morning. Gerald, the security guard, was standing up in the gazebo keeping everyone away from the place until the Okaloosa County deputies arrived, but he had dashed over while Gerald was turned away talking with someone.

He wished for weeks that he hadn't done it for she was a bloody mess and the gulls were pecking out what was left of her eyes. The eye sockets were just strings of blood roping their way down her cheeks. She didn't have any arms from about the elbows down and what was left was wrapped in Pigglyl Wiggly sacks. "Hell," he thought, "I didn't even know that Piggly Wiggly supermarkets were this far South."

He remembered he had been drinking that morning just like this now and that he threw up all over the beach just like that beach attendant had.

He took another swig out of the long necked bottle of tequila he clutched in his right hand and thought, "What the Hell? This year wasn't filled with bodies, but What the Hell was that cat? And where the Hell is that snake he heard about?"

He laughed, almost giggled, as he thought how his little daughter Kiera had named the cat Poseidon.

He had the strong urge to pee so he pulled his shorts down and they fell around his ankles as he stood pissing into the Gulf. "Don't be a Phony, dude. You tell the kids not to pee in the pool and here you are peeing in the big pool. You Phony, you."

As he stumbled across the sand trying to pull his shorts up, he started acting out one of Bert and Ernie's skits that his youngest daughter, Natalie, was learning. He ran weaving across the sand with his shorts half way up hollering 'Near' and then turned and ran in the other direction hollering 'Far' and laughing till he collapsed onto the sand.

The bottle was about empty he saw as he held it up still clutching it tightly and he thought he should go back to the condo for a refill. As he walked from the west toward the gazebo he saw something several feet out in the water that was being pulled quickly away from him.

"I gonna be a frigging hero!" he shouted. He plunged out into the water doing a belly flop and coming up spitting water aiming to catch whatever it was.

Al's body caught in a fair size wave and turned face toward him and came crashing into him. He yelled, fell backward into the next wave and struggled against the riptide to get loose and make it back to shore. Stinking sour tequila came spurting out as he stumbled head-long across the sand toward the gazebo.

When he thought he was safe from it, he turned and could barely make it out through the fog which wasn't even beginning to lift; it had a string of fish around its neck and a blue crab had already attached itself to one of the man's cheeks.

He threw up again or tried too, made his way up the ramp to the gazebo, and fell onto one of the long wooden benches inside.

He awoke from what he thought was a nightmare. Standing up in the gazebo peering out into the fog which was even thicker it seemed, he didn't see anything. A lone pelican swept by him not fifteen feet in front of where he stood and he jumped back and cussed as it flew into the fog going west.

The pelican must have knocked some sense into his mind because he decided that he would not say anything about what had happened to him down here on the beach—not even to his wife, Kelly. She wouldn't believe him anyway.

He didn't realize he had only slept fifteen minutes or so, or he might have spread the word about Al's body. He headed back toward their condo.

He passed Daniel Sheraton as he was walking down toward the beach.

29

Men at times are masters of their fates

Henry Embser had worked for Sun Setter Beach Service for four years starting when he was a senior at Collegiate High School over at Niceville. He was an Eagle Scout, an all-around, all-American good guy that every girl's mother wants as a son-in-law, and as a twenty-three-old he was Daniel Sheraton's best and most trusted beach attendant.

I walked back out onto my balcony with my coffee and some scrambled eggs and toast, saw that I still couldn't see anything much except the sidewalk down by the pool because the fog blocked everything else, but then Daniel Sheraton appeared out of the white wall.

As he walked down the boardwalk toward the gazebo, I spoke to him, "Good morning,"

He was startled and he may have jumped a little but he never would have admitted it.

"Gee, I didn't see you Prof," he answered loud enough for me to hear.

"Stay alert out there! That darn cat may be hungry."

He laughed as he talked to me from down the boardwalk, "You know this fog will be gone by ten, so maybe I'll just sleep till then. We're sure won't have any customers in this soupy mess. Henry got caught behind a wreck, so he'll be late."

He walked on down the ramp and disappeared into the fog.

Daniel was thinking how much herding all the young men who worked for him must be like tending to a preschool class, or maybe trying to catch up with a pod of dolphin by trying to think where they would be going next as they went under the water. The Prof had told him once about a bunch of kayakers who tried to keep up with a pod right out here in front of the gazebo.

He thought he should just close down everything and go fishing. I'll just send all the guys back home and go over throw a line off the dock back of Debbie's house across the Blvd from the La Mancha in the Sound or I might really go fishing and just run off up to Black River Park for the day and fish for trout, he thought. Then he knew he wouldn't because he needed to work today and so did his boys for the season was nearly over.

He wasn't angry at Henry at all for that was not part of his personality and besides, he was soon-to-be a new father of the son he had always wanted—Dylan Sheraton—and that was really what was on his mind this morning.

He walked past the pole where they hung the flags announcing the conditions of the water for the day. He couldn't see the water from where he was but heard 'lappers' hitting the sand. Weather this morning had indicated that there was a riptide and he knew the water would be calm except for that current pulling away from the beach.

As most of his crew always were, he was barefooted. Walking over to the big box that stored the umbrellas and beach chairs during the night he stretched up to unlock the lock on top of the box. He slid the door over along the side of the box and reached in to take umbrellas off the top of the stack.

As he was carrying six or eight of them down to where he stabbed them into the sand in a line along the shore, he heard Henry coming down the boardwalk.

"Sorry, Boss, Henry hollered," and they both laughed for it was a given between Daniel and all his guys that no one called him 'Boss.'

"That's alright, you have just been docked an hour for being late," he said as he reached into to take a beach chair off the stack.

The snake coiled up in the corner of the box left of the door had been aroused when Daniel had slid a chair off the stack. There was no warning rattle for Eva had torn its rattles off. It struck with all the force it had left biting into Daniel's ankle and sinking its fangs into the soft part in the back. Daniel threw the chair aside, yelled with pain, and fell onto the ground.

The snake fell from his ankle and coiled to strike again, but suddenly there was a growl and hiss that Daniel and Henry would later say sounded like some primitive beast. Both of them hollered out in surprise as Poseidon leaped out of the fog; his aim was perfect as he locked his teeth just behind the rattler's head and starting beating it into the sand. He and the big six foot snake rolled and tumbled across the sand until once again, they were up close to the front of the box. The big cat, never turning lose, started whacking the snake against the side of the box.

Poseidon must have lost some of his grip for about a foot of the snake was hanging out of his mouth now and it struck at Poseidon latching onto one of his powerful shoulders.

Three or four minutes later with a final burst of power, Poseidon had crushed the snake's body. Finally the snake was hanging limp in Poseidon's mouth. He turned and trotted off through the fog toward the Air Command. When the area was searched latter, not a bit of the snake was found.

Henry hadn't only been watching what was happening, but had been busy since it all started. He had his cell phone out and call 911 before Poseidon had leaped out of the fog.

He had never seen Daniel scared before and he understood. He took over as Daniel lay on the sand yelling and Henry saw that tears filled

137

his eyes and he was saying he would never see his boy grow up. The only hint of humor Henry felt was that he knew Daniel would never admit later how he had reacted.

He knew Daniel had to calm down, and do it quickly. Even though he heard the ER vehicle racing down Santa Rose Blvd with its siren blaring from the Fire Station up at the end of the Blvd where it meets Highway 98, Henry knew that he must act quickly.

He sat down next to Daniel's head, grabbed him against his will and lifted him up off the sand and scooped sand up under his back with his free hand. He put his knee behind Daniel's shoulder and raised him up almost into a sitting position so his heart would be higher than the snakebite on his ankle.

"Hope none of the guys see us like this, Boss," he said trying to get Daniel's attention.

"You just lost another hour's pay."

Then they both laughed and Henry felt Daniel's body relax, but It seemed forever before he saw the ER crew running down toward him and it was after they lifted Daniel onto a gurney and rushed back across the sand that he realized his own heart was beating harder than he could remember.

This time I rushed to the sliding glass door and slid it open for many of us had heard the yelling coming from the beach and all of us had heard the siren as the ER truck came toward us. I rushed back in my condo, through the front door, and hurried to the elevator. It took me two or three minutes to get around to where the ER attendants were carrying Daniel up the ramp to the gazebo. He looked at me and said, "You were right, Prof, that darn cat was hungry." I felt good for if he could make jokes at a time like this, he would be all right.

Henry had saved Daniel's life and a few days later when he visited him in Sacred Heart Hospital, Daniel squeezed his arm real tight.

"Do I get the two hour's pay back," he laughed.

"Yep."

Once again just like last year, most of the guests checked out the morning after the rattlesnake bite Daniel.

Bette was fit to be tied as she had no idea what to do. A J almost got fired when he remarked, "Well that damn cat was good for something." Bette was not in a good mood. Craig and his crew searched high and low for any sign of the snake. The Okaloosa County deputies arrived and questioned Reverend Crabtree and the two women that were still at the La Mancha, but they convinced the police they didn't know anything about the snake. They all swore they didn't know where Eva was as they hadn't seen her since yesterday. Bette tried to get them to leave but Crabtree threatened to sue the complex because he was an owner like all the other owners.

Gladis found Poseidon's body a few days later tangled up in a thick vine that grows underneath where a big section of the ugly chain link fence was ripped halfway down from the top. When it was examined later, five snake bites were found in various places.

As we sat around gossiping one night that week, we invariably turned our conversation to that cat. Bicycle Bob took a big draw from the straw that always sticks into his big plastic glass full of White Russians, "You all know why that cat was here?"

Gladis fell for it and said, "No, why?"

"That damn spectral beast appeared out on our beach and pestered us for only one reason—to have rattlesnake for breakfast."

There was silence for a second and Bob burst into one of his loud rowdy laughs.

30

Another Body on the Beach

About a week after that drunk woke up down at the beach and decided he would keep his mouth shut about seeing a body floating out from the beach with a string of fish around its neck and Daniel Sheraton had been bitten by the rattlesnake at the gazebo, J C Blevins got a call from a Major on Eglin Air Base. They had become acquainted last summer when so much was happening at the La Mancha and since it is up against Eglin's beach fence, the Major had become involved also.

The Major told J C that a man's body had washed up on Eglin's beach about a quarter of a mile west of the La Mancha, and wondered if J C could come see the body and maybe identify it. J C went to the morgue on Eglin and knew that it was Al Dollar's body as soon as the body bag had been unzipped. He had interview Al last summer at the La Mancha when that first body had washed up just below the gazebo.

The days after Al's partially eaten body was found with part of a string of fish still around his neck and a snake bit on his cheek that Doc Wells concluded was the actual cause of his death were horrible for Gladis.

I had tried to walk with Al on occasion but was unable to keep up with his pace, but Gladis walked with him almost every day. He would appear at her patio door at about the same time in late afternoon and they would make four or five trips around the Dolphin, across the parking lot, around the Pelican and down to the gazebo maybe to pause for a minute, and then on around the big pool to Gladis's patio where they started all over again.

We sat there two nights later at the pool and decided we knew very little about him until his death. He had been very important down at Cocoa

Beach during the early days of America's mission into space and later on at Brandenburg when the Shuttle program was so important. So, he was entitled to be buried at Arlington with his Lieutenant Colonel ranking in the Air Force.

Bob had said, "He would say save your money," and all of us agreed Al would think we were foolish to journey up Virginia for we wouldn't be allowed on the grounds of the Cemetery, so we celebrated Al's time with us as the sun set. We toasted him drinking vodka and water which was his drink of choice.

My cell phone rang at about five o'clock the next morning. I saw it was Gladis calling. I dreaded talking to her because the previous evening as the group of us sat around the pool, she had cried and left us just after the first toast to Al.

I answered my phone, "Yes, Gladis? Is everything alright?"

"I just thought maybe I would walk with you this morning. I have a favor though. Why don't we walk Al's route this morning instead of you walking down on the beach?"

"Sure, I'll be over in a few minutes."

I hung up and the coffee had brewed in the maker, so I grabbed a cup and went to the elevator. I dreaded seeing her and walking with her for I knew she wouldn't make the walk without crying.

We walked, but we didn't talk, and on the second circle around the buildings she walked through the sliding glass door of her condo and shut it without saying a word.

31

At High Tide

They met at the popular seafood and oyster bar at the demand of the larger man. The High Tide has been here for years and is a favorite for tourists who return each year and especially the locals who know the food will always be good and plentiful. Besides that, they have the best oysters-on-the-half-shell in the Panhandle.

Celeste seated them in the room adjacent to the bar at the request of the one she recognized for he was a good customer.

Only two other customers were in the little room which is used primarily for private parties as they were seated and by the time their drinks and the first two dozen oysters arrived, those other customers were finished and had gone.

"We've got to get something straight before you get yourself killed. I mean literally before you get yourself killed.... Understand? I am the boss up here and you were brought up here for one reason, well I guess two reasons."

The other one squirmed in his seat and took a big gulp of the beer he had ordered.

"You have caused quite a diversion at the La Mancha and that's good."

The other one almost smiled as the large man continued.

"But you have for some reason decided to take things into your own hands. Why the Hell you killed Walkin Al is just crazy. And then you had to be some kind of gangster and put a string of fish around his neck. Why?"

"I thought it would lead people astray."

"If you hadn't been such a hair brained idiot, no one would know that he didn't die of a snake bite. But, Damn It, you had to string dead fish around his neck. Where the Hell did you get those fish? You didn't lead people astray—you just told everybody that he was murdered. You idiot."

"I thought he would be eaten by something out there in the water because the riptide was pulling him out and I thought he would just keep going."

"Well, he didn't and now you have really caused us a problem. That's what happened to Ollie when he went on that shooting spree down Santa Rosa Blvd. We couldn't have the publicity for such a stunt, and you know what happened to him. Right?"

He leaned in until his forehead was almost touching the other's head. "Well, you do, don't you?"

The other one quietly said, "Yes."

"Good, now that we have things defined and know what the consequences are for screwing up things, there are two things I need you to do and then you are finished up here."

A look of 'well that's over' spread over the smaller man's face.

"First, you are to take care of Eva. Do it however you want, but if you involve me or if you attract attention, you will…. Well, you know what will happen."

"Why Eva? Can't she just leave?"

"Hell, no, she knows too much. She overstepped what she was supposed to do too. Why the hell did she bring that fuckin snake? Who the hell goes around with a rattlesnake in their cooler? God, you all are idiots."

"Okay, okay, I'll get it done and not draw attention to anyone."

"And the other thing you are to do is what you were hired to do in the first place. Swim over there and take care of it. Do it in the next two days."

"Okay, that job will be a pleasure and easy too."

"Get that done and you can leave. Just vacate the two condos at the La Mancha and don't do anything else. Just leave. All right? Now, do you want another dozen oysters?"

They sat at the table for a long time talking about what was going on down in Miami, how three or four college football teams were doing everything right and who should be number one; they even bet $10 on an upcoming game between two teams. They talked a while about the dumb things Schaberg was pulling in the courtroom, how Launie had to know she was not going to win this trial nor the next one if there was a next one, and how they might have to eliminate Sam Ripley and Alice Pearl.

Finally the big man asked for their check, paid the bill with cash, and left Celeste another fifty dollar tip.

32

Daniel fishing on the bank of the Sound

Just as few days after the snake had shot a heavy load of venom into his ankle and he had put Henry Embser in charge of the rest of his crew, Daniel sat on the back deck of a friend's house just across the Blvd from the La Mancha. He had his fishing line in the water and was almost dozing off but the outlandish events of this summer were even worse than last year's and he couldn't get them out of his mind.

He thought he sure would be glad when the season was over and he could spend the winter with Lyn and their new son. All summer long for several years, he worked seven days a week and he wanted this season to end.

He wanted to say words that he heard every day, except he never cursed, and also knew he needed the money to make it through the winter. When he had talked to Henry last night, Henry told him a long paddle board was missing from the stack they kept at the La Mancha.

He felt a tug on his line and about five minutes later had a filthy no good catfish flopping on the deck before him. Ignoring the pain in his left ankle he leaned over, pulled the hook from its mouth, and kicked the thing back into the water with his right foot.

Something caught his eye as he looked up toward Egg Island to the west. A brightly colored object had floated around the island and was drifting down toward him. He watch and then exclaimed, "What the heck?"

Coming straight along the bank was his lost paddle board with Sun Setter stamped on its bottom. He could see it for it was upside-down and floating low in the water. As it went by him he saw that several bungie cords were holding something against the board. It had to be heavy for the board which usually bounces along on top the water was nearly under water.

He quickly got his cell phone off the table next to him and called 911. He was surprised when J C Blevins answer his call and in just a couple of minutes, he saw a water patrol boat pull out from the dock underneath the jail.

J C waved at him and Daniel saw J C bring the boat up alongside the floating board. The young woman with J C on the boat snagged the board with a hook and Daniel saw her secured it to a gunnel on the boat.

J C gave Daniel a courtesy call about an hour later and told him a young woman's body had been fastened to the board. She had obviously been dead when she was fastened to it for there was a bullet hole in the middle of her forehead and no hole in the board.

No one at the police station knew who she was. He also said, "I'll have to hold your board until we investigate this."

None of Daniel's crew had ever heard him cuss, but when he was off the phone with Blevins if they had been around they would have.

33

Lollipop lollipop, oh lolli lolli lolli – Pop

He sat on the rough boards that are what remains of the Fort Walton Beach Landing behind the new jail with his cell phone to his ear. Across the Sound he saw the lights of the La Mancha and the outline of the big house on Tarpon Street. Launie's big yacht, the *Lollipop,* is anchored a few feet away as it has been since she was arrested; it sloshes in the water as he waited for an answer.

A voice says, "Pop?"

He answers, "lollipop lollipop, oh lolli lolli lolli – Pop."

The voice laughs.

With halfhearted laugh he replies, "Great song for the story."

The voice says, "How's the script coming along?"

"We can't find our lead man. We have people all over town searching for the right one—inside and out, but we can't find him."

"Listen, and I speak for the director, if you don't find him and let him play his part, you are going take his part in the final act."

"Damn it, I doing all I can to find the right one. I know an old woman who lives with her dog that might be the answer."

"Well, get her and make the script good."

J C Blevins and Marvin sat in the parking lot of the pancake house a few hundred yards away and listened to the conversation on the bugged phone of the man who sat on the Landing.

"What do you make of that?" Blevins was laughing for the first time in weeks as he had been so stressed about Ester and how the trial was dragging along. "Did you ever hear anything so ridiculous? Sounds like some three year olds talking on the phone and not wanting their folks to understand what they're talking about."

"Sounds like an amateur production of an easy code to me," Marvin answered, "But we better get Judge Boyd and put her in a safe place. They are obviously looking for Chuck because they know he is the real witness to all Launie Sanderson's dealings and will hang several people down in Miami where that voice is coming from."

Blevins agreed, "I keep having to move those two, Sam Ripley and Alice Pearl, from what we think is a safe house because I'm always thinking someone is following me as I take them provisions, so Judge Boyd might not be any safer if we find her a place."

"We need to get them all and take them to Eglin—that's the safest place around where they will be guarded by guards 24/7," Marvin answered.

They parted, Blevins going down Highway 98 toward Mary Ester to persuade Judge Boyd that she needed protection and Marvin headed north on Highway 85 to talk with the commander of Eglin to find a place to protect their witnesses and the judge.

34

Bad Dog, Bad Morning

Judge Boyd had a headache, something she almost never had for she still followed the teachings of her mother's people and faced east each morning to sprinkle ground-up maize in front of her open doorway and ask for a blessing way for her day. When her husband and best friend had died last year, she had gone to the humane shelter and picked out a feisty Australian Sheep dog named Coxy. She had wondered about the name but was told the former owner who could no longer take care of it had named it Coxey. She was beginning to understand why the former owner couldn't take care of the dog for Coxy was into everything—one minor disaster to the next. This morning when Coxy had exited through the doggy door for her morning inspection of the property and potty trip Judge Boyd had hollered after her, "Hurry and come back for breakfast for I have to leave. And stay out of trouble!"

As she dressed and washed her smooth almost unlined face, she heard a loud splash from the direction of the Sound. She hurried through the front door and saw Coxy struggling to get back up the steep bank to the yard. She ran to the edge of the bank and realized she would have to get down on her hands and knees to reach the dog. As she was pulling Coxy's front legs up to her, she lost her balance and her arms plunged into the dark water of the Sound getting her blouse and light coat wet.

After much splashing and with Coxy wiggling so she couldn't control her, she got the dog and herself up into the yard and thought, "This is a bad omen for the day I think." She took the squirming dog in and put her in the room that had her water dispenser, scolded the dog, closed the door behind her, and went in to regroup. She tried to call J C Blevins and tell him what had happened but his phone went straight to voice mail. She left a message that she would be late.

149

As she pull her mini Cooper out of the lane which ran down to her house on to Highway 98, she was surprised to see a police car get in right behind her and recognized J C Blevins as the driver. He actually flashed his blue lights at her and she pulled into the first turn-off she found.

When he walked up along her driver's door, she said, "I just left you a message on your phone and why in the world are you following me?"

"I was coming to get you anyway for we have rumors that you are being watched so someone can find where you are keeping Chuck during your hearing."

"What do you mean? You think Chuck is in danger? And me too?"

"Yes, we do. They want me to move you to a safe place."

"Well, I won't go and that is final. Moving those two eye witnesses don't seem to do any good for you are always concerned about their safety. Oh, Mr. Blevins, I apologize. I should not have said that. But, I won't move," she said as she pulled back onto the highway and headed for the jail.

Mary Ester, the quiet little residential town which adjoins Fort Walton Beach to the west is about ten or fifteen minutes from the Okaloosa County jail where Chuck was being held as she heard his trial.

She was in her usual happy and pleasant mood by the time she arrived there for she had a way of settling everything in her mind so that her mood was even and her thinking straight when she arrived and she took the elevator to the third floor where she had set-up court in one of the conference rooms.

She had firmly told trooper Blevins she would not move and that she didn't want anyone posted to watch her house. Besides that, she reasoned, anyone could just hang around the jail and watch her routine from there. It was a silly matter and she closed her mind to it. Her main concern was for Chuck and to get his trail settled so he could get back to his life in Chicago.

Mr. Porter had given her two very efficient law students who were working in the Prosecuting Attorney's Office this semester. She had decided to 'give' one of them to Chuck to help him with his testimony and use the other to help her with the paperwork that was stacking up. She had proven to Chuck that she was fair and unbiased as she got to know him, even going so far as to let him pick which one of the two students he wanted. He took Benjamin Marshall and she was please that she retained Alyx Vigil.

Both Alyx and Benjamin were somewhat surprised when they realized they were being a part of a very important trial and very unusual trial. Just like the people in Fort Walton Beach and the surrounding community who read the *NorthWest Daily*, they had never known about so important a trial being decided by only a judge. Judge Boyd was distress the entire afternoon when she read the paper and it divulged that Chuck was back in Fort Walton Beach and being held somewhere. There was nothing she could do about it, so she got on with the business of his hearing.

The two law students spent a lot of time together usually having lunch together every day. Ben was surprised to find out that Alyx was from Rancho de Rio Grande which is a little village next to Albuquerque. He knew Judge Boyd's connection to New Mexico and wondered if the Judge knew that Alyx was from there. He and Alyx talked about it and decided to not mention it to the Judge. Ben was also surprised that he would spend the semester next to so beautiful young lady—irony he thought, a beautiful famous Judge and an equally beautiful companion.

Judge Boyd had decided the entire hearing, as she called it, would be held in an informal atmosphere with her sitting on one side of the conference table with Alyx next to her and Chuck facing her from the other side with Ben next to him. During the weeks, she decided that an armed guard was not necessary outside the conference room door. She convinced Mr. Porter to take the guard away as he was just calling attention to that room as he stood there. But this morning, the guard was back and anyone could see he was carrying several guns.

She had read all of Chuck's declaration last night and wanted to ask him several questions today starting with how he had picked up the drugs that were being dropped in the Gulf.

"I would take the big yacht out and Launie would sometimes be watching from the shore—at the state park pavilion or from the condo she rented at the Four Corners Hotel that faced the Gulf. She always had notification that a package was about to arrive. Then when I spotted a bundle in the water, I would snag it with a hook and bring it back in to the little dock behind the Dorm. I would leave it on board the *Lollipop* and from there I don't know what happened to it."

Ben had laughed when Chuck said the name of the yacht and Judge Boyd asked him what was funny.

"It's such a sophomoric joke," Ben answered.

"I don't understand why," Judge Boyd replied. "But, I don't care either, so Chuck, did you ever see a boat of any kind out on the water that might have made the drop?"

"There were always many boats out in the Gulf in front of the La Mancha for it is a very good fishing place, I hear. I did observe the water out there one time for several days but I never recognized the same boat coming and going—except for the charter fishing boats which were out there every day. But they usually went out several miles further than where I would find the bundles in the water."

"We may come back to that, but now I want you to tell me about when you went to all those banks to clean out Launie's safety deposit boxes.

I read what you wrote to me in you declaration, but I want you to repeat it to me."

"Well, Launie had given me authority to get into those boxes one day when she was about half-drunk and when we had that big fight about...about... Ma'am, I'm sorry. Will you let us take a break so I can get myself...?"

"No, I want you to tell me just as you are feeling it right now."

"I was so upset with her for she didn't care if Joe had... Had disappeared into the Gulf out there and was surely dead. All she was concerned about was that someone would find his body and call attention to the place where the drugs were usually dropped. She just wanted me to go back and find him for that reason."

"So, the two of you started hitting and slapping each other."

"Yes, Ma'am. I had never done anything like that before. I always did as she told me. I would never slap and hit around on a woman either. But I was so mad. We sat there and hit and hit and hit each other. I realized in a split second that the next time I hit her, it would really injure her, so I shoved her away and as I went out the door I took the little box that had the keys to the bank boxes in it."

"You went to all the banks and got the money. What did you find in one of the boxes? You know what I am referring to."

"It just happened to be the last box. Inside it were Joe's and my birth certificates. That was the first time I knew what my last name really was."

"What did you do then?"

"I took the certificates and wrote a note on a piece of paper, but it into the box, and left the bank."

"Okay, now I want you to clearly and carefully tell me what you wrote in that note."

"I said I was taking the money even though I figure she would have any trouble filling up all those boxes again and that I was going somewhere and using the money to help people."

"You are sure you said you didn't want the money for yourself?"

"Yes. I'm sure."

"Okay, now I'm sending you back to your lovely home in that cell back there while Alyx, Ben, and I set a trap."

"You are setting a trap? For who?"

"Well, the grammar I learned says it should be 'for whom?' and I don't want to tell you right now. If it works, we are all in great danger and if it doesn't we are all still in that great danger."

Chuck looked squarely at Judge Boyd and saw in her eyes that she was serious and that she wasn't going to divulge another thing to him, so he turned and walked out the conference room door and down to his cell. He opened the door and went in and sat down on his twin bed and it suddenly hit him that the door was not locked and he could leave if he wanted and also anyone could walk in on him at any time. He felt very defenseless and wondered if this was part of Judge Boyd's trap.

35

Tripped again, but he doesn't know it

"Alyx, I want you to take this to Mr. Porter's office and wait for him until he returns from wherever he might be. He's probably in court but he might be anywhere. I don't want you to give this envelope to anyone else—not to any of his assistants. I don't even want anyone to know that you have this message I'm sending to him. Just say that I'm sending you and have instructed you to meet and talk with no one else but him."

She handed Alyx the envelope and her mind was whirling around wondering if she was doing the right thing sending this young woman with such a message, but she knew she couldn't risk calling Curtis Porter for she now realized just what danger she and the three involved with Chuck's case were in.

She felt almost sick at her stomach and sensed she was way outside her normal blessed way, but she had to send Ben on what might be even a more dangerous errand, "Ben, I want you to find J C Blevins who is probably in court in Judge Bickel's courtroom, wait until there is a recess and that will probably not be too long if things run as they have been, and tell Mr. Blevins that I sent you and want him to get you to Marvin as quickly as he can. He will know who Marvin is and Marvin will know why I am sending you to him. Marvin will give you a message for me that I do not want Mr. Blevins to hear."

She looked at her cell phone and saw that it was almost lunch time and with any luck, Bickel's court would be taking a lunch recess, but she was really surprised when not more than fifteen minutes later, Curtis Porter walked into the conference room where she sat.

She explained the news she had heard from Chuck as she questioned him this morning, and asked if she could hold the most important piece of information until they heard or met with Marvin.

Then she threw both Porter and Alyx as big jolt as she said to Porter, "Mr. Porter, I want to put Alyx on a plane to Albuquerque where I want her to stay until all this mess is settled and I want to send Ben to Corpus Christi to his folks for just as long. Don't try to tell me you will find a safe place for them around here for I won't listen to you"

Alyx looked stunned and Porter answered, "I'll have to trust your judgment, Judge Boyd. We'll have tickets for both of them in an hour. Now, we need to find Marvin and meet with Chuck together. Alyx, you get your belongings together quietly and meet me in my office. They will know what you are to do."

Ben had been successful and Marvin appeared in the doorway. Porter explained to Ben what he wanted him to do, and he hurried away to get his bag packed for the trip.

Marvin asked, "What is this all about, Judge Boyd?"

"Marvin, I know that you are working as hard as anyone can to solve how so much drugs are getting into the Panhandle of our state. I helped you several times when I was an active judge to get subpoenas and court orders, but now I think I have something that will help you even more. But, we are going to have to trust Chuck to be square with us. I think he will."

They walked down the hallway to the room where Chuck as staying and Marvin was the one who exclaimed, "This door isn't even locked. What in the world?"

"That's entirely my fault as I took away the guard and trusted Chuck to go back to his room on his own. It was a silly mistake on my part. I need to retire," Judge Boyd answered. They all laughed.

Curtis Porter was not as forgiving of her as he blurted out, "But that isn't the reason I'm upset. First of all, he is a prisoner of the county and most of all there would be no way for him to know if someone walked into his cell until it was too late.

"Mr. Porter, I'm truly at fault and realized how gullible I have been."

Chuck was surprised as the three enter his little room, "I hope the three of you being here is not a bad omen."

"Now, Chuck, I want you to tell Mr. Porter and Marvin what you left in the last of the eight bank boxes you emptied before you left Fort Walton Beach."

"I wrote a note saying that no doubt Launie would succeed in getting all those boxes filled up again, but that I was taking the money to do some good somewhere."

Judge Boyd looked at Porter and Marvin and saw that each of them realized the importance of what Chuck had just said.

Porter was the first to speak, "Schaberg was issued a power of attorney to look in all those bank boxes. We got a subpoena to inspect them after he had been to all the banks and there was no note in any of the boxes. Are you certain, Chuck, about the note?"

"I'll swear to it in court."

Marvin interjected, "Oh God, I hope it doesn't' come to that or you are a marked man." He looked sheepishly at Chuck and said, "But you must know, you already are."

"The point is that Schaberg knows all about the drug dealing that Launie was doing. He knows and still he is defending her in Bickel's court.

He must be instructed by someone really powerful to be following like a sheep," Judge Boyd said.

"Bickel has said time and again that the trial going on right now is only for the murder of Ollie, and I have wondered why he keeps repeating that to Schaberg and me when he has us meet at the bench," Porter said.

"Well, we've got to get Chuck out of here. I mean away from here. Can't you make a ruling on what he is going to have to pay for and get him out of here?" Marvin asked Judge Boyd.

"Yes, I will this afternoon."

Chuck felt the pit of his stomach drop and wonder what he would be doing tomorrow.

36

Going Home

The bus pulled into the station on Perry Street and Chuck loaded his gear into the luggage compartment under the bus and got on to find a seat which would be on the Gulf side as the bus went down Highway 98 toward Pensacola. The five o'clock traffic had made its reckless way through the narrow streets and the sun was setting out over the water as he looked out the window. As the bus passed in front of the jail where he had been for the last few weeks, he saw the La Mancha across the Sound behind it and a tinge of happiness hit him for he had been allowed to tell the Prof he was leaving.

"Will I be hearing from you again?" the old man had asked.

"I'm not supposed to have anything to do with Okaloosa County for the rest of my life but a postcard from somewhere to you would be hard to trace to me."

"Not if it had a red car on it."

"The car is gone. It's going to be hard to explain to Katie how I'm coming home on a bus and that we don't have a car anymore, but Judge Boyd knew that would be the thing that bothered me most. She said that prized possessions taken away leads to humility and soul searching and she is right. I've grown very fond of that lady just as I have of you, sir. She didn't say anything about the bank account you have to help kids with and she didn't say anything about the account in the same bank that belongs to Ester Haynes. I got off easy Prof. All I have to do is keep my nose clean for five years and to continue to help others."

"Neither of those will be hard for you as you already have learned that."

"I wish you all the happiness possible and hope that the world around the La Mancha might settle down and get back to normal."

"I wish you the same but I have my doubts about things getting back to normal around here."

From the bus window he saw a lone gull flying out a few yards from the shore and it seemed to be racing the bus he imagined. Surely it wasn't the Prof's bird Jonathan telling him goodbye. He smiled as he realized he is getting as bad as the Prof—talking to birds.

He was so glad it was over. He felt something in his mind about leaving Launie behind for she was in spite of everything, his mother, but he couldn't decide what the feeling was—just an empty vacant place he decided. He was leaving behind all the hurt and grieving he had known. He didn't think he would ever come back to Fort Walton Beach again but he knew that he would have to sneak back some night for here was where Joe is and also Ollie. No, he thought for he was going back to Katie and a life like he had never had before—a life of peace and giving and love.

He thought of something the Prof had said once and someone had repeated that Sunday afternoon as they all sat on the Prof's balcony, 'In the worst tragedies ever written or lived, innocent people have been caught up in the scheme of things and sometimes those innocent ones become heroes if they can escape' but the Prof was wrong in a way for no one can ever escape himself, Chuck thought.

He saw the waves crashing into the shore during a long stretch where the Sound was narrow enough so the Gulf could be seen from the road and thought he could almost hear them through the thick window. He closed his eyes and gave thanks that there were still people like the Prof, Judge Boyd, Ester Haynes, and J C Blevins who cared about people and tried to do the right thing. He gave thanks that the Creator of all had used the water to mean so much to humans and he remembered another thing the Prof had said once, 'The waves either crash into the shore with a show of the great power of the Gulf, or they hardly touch the Island at all with a gentleness that is very calming; always changing, ever mysterious' and Chuck thought, isn't that what life is?

He snuggled down into the pillow he had bought that afternoon and tried to sleep for it was a long bus ride to Chicago. He would make it because he knew Katie was there waiting for him.

37

The fog

I heard voices shouting in anger and suddenly a body topples over the railing of an upper floor balcony of the Sea Shell building—it appeared to be either the fifth or sixth floor. It hit the ground but I could barely hear it as it sounded like a floppy wet mattress hitting the thick spongy thick grass below.

I stopped dead in my tracks as I realize we probably have another death at the La Mancha. Oh, God, no, I thought. Damn, we just found Walkin Al's body three weeks ago up a half mile or so on the beach toward Navarre, and now another one?

Because of Al's death and all the commotion that it caused, I have begun walking the trail up along Santa Rosa Blvd. When I got out of bed this morning, Skipper, grunted his disapproval and a few minutes later when I stood down on the sidewalk beneath my balcony he stuck his lopsided head through the railing and barked at me. I probably should have turned right around and gone back up to bed for the fog was so thick this November morning that I could only see a few feet in front of me. I headed north along the sidewalk, went through the guard shack entrance where I said 'Good Morning' to Gerald and got a strange look back from him, and walked east on to the walking path next to the west bound lane of Santa Rosa Blvd.

Now I was coming back after going almost a mile down toward the Thumb.

And now this. We have evil all around us I think, and it's too damn nerve-wracking for an old man like me. Rattlesnakes and spectral cats from the Gulf and a weird preacher with his harem. What in the world is happening?

We didn't need anything more than Launie's trial and Fort Walton Beach is filled with absurd tales, gossip, and intriguing clues as to why she killed Ollie. Most of them are foreign to me and I sit in the courtroom every day.

Until Al's death, the La Mancha complex had been somewhat spared this time, but too many local people know that the many deaths of the summer of 2014 were all connected with the La Mancha and now Gerald and the rest of the crew have to stop many cars from coming onto the property when they pull up to the little guard house at the entrance. Gerald gets most of them for most of them seem to come at night. Lyndell, his boss, has hired another security patrol lady that we see walking the property lots of nights.

But that really doesn't stop gawkers or anyone else—even someone who is up to no good—from getting onto the property. All anyone needs to do is park at one of the many public beach accesses along the Blvd and walk down the beach to our beachfront for that's exactly what happened when Skipper and I got shot by the crossbow. Strange that a year later I would find out in court from Ester Haynes that it was Ollie who shot us and he did it because he was terrified of dogs and Skipper had barked at him one day.

And just now as I heard the shouting and saw the body fall, I did what I have since it happened, clutch my hand as I feel the pain in my right wrist where one of the arrows had gone entirely through my wrist.

No one seemed to be roused out of bed by the argument I had heard nor see what happened because no lights come on and I don't see anyone out on a balcony. That's strange I thought for it is so quiet this morning.

As the body fell, I thought I saw an arm reach out to grab or push it, but in the dark with the fog so thick, I couldn't be sure what was happening or be certain if I had seen an arm pulled back quickly. There was something strange about the body too for it looked like the head was hanging loosely to one side like the neck was broken. I was at least fifty yards from where cars can turn off the Blvd into the La Mancha and it all happened suddenly and quickly so I was not sure what I saw.

I had pulled out my cell phone and dialed 911 probably so fast the body had hardly hit the ground. I gave my name and told what happened and seconds later, I heard a siren start from the SUV the county deputies drive as they went wailing down Highway 98 from the jail just across the Sound. I could see the flashing light spasmodically as it broke through patches of fog. I heard it cross over Brooks Bridge and make the sharp right turn on the Blvd. It would be here in two or three minutes.

Suddenly, a pick-up screeched forward as it had been parked along the Blvd beside the Sea Oats building. It jerked and then veered across the median and headed straight toward me and even though I jumped to one side as fast as I could it swerved into me. A sharp pain swept through me as I went flying into some thick shrubs planted beside the street.

*

"What the hell? You hit that old man. Didn't you see him?."

"Yeah, did it on purpose. Didn't you see who it was? That old teacher who lives in Pelican who sees and knows too fuckin much. He's always watching me and if we are about to meet he turns and goes in a different direction." She raised her voice and almost shouted, "Don't you hear that siren coming toward us. I have to get off the street fast. I just cut across the median and there he was. An absolute bulls-eye."

She laughed as the other woman shouted, "Hurry, we can make it—there's Tarpon Drive right there. That police car is almost here."

The pick-up careened around the corner onto Tarpon Drive and the driver turned out the lights. In the rear view mirror, she saw the flashing lights of the police SUV as it zipped past. She breather a little easier as the two of them crouched down in the seat.

"We've got to get this done" No one will ever suspect us. We'll get this done, Levi Crabtree or whatever his name really is will be out of our lives, and we can leave in the morning."

With the lights still off, she drove the pick-up into the drive closest to the Sound. One of them opened the tail gate and they pulled the body from the pick-up bed.

"This bastard won't be slurping around on either of us again. Good God, why did we ever again to get into this mess? I don't give a rat's ass who he is with the bunch down in Miami, I through playing a trampoline."

"Just like everything else we've always done—the money. I sure as shit didn't know that rattlesnakes were going to be involved though. Where do you think Eva got that slithering thing? I hate snakes and to think it got lose."

Struggling together, they drug the Reverend Levi Crabtree's body between them down the bank where a boat was waiting with its motor running. Because his neck was broken, they had a hard time keeping his head upright as it kept falling on one or the other's shoulder.

The boat pulled away from the bank and the driver turned it to the west. About a quarter of a mile west of the La Mancha and just across the Sound a little on west from the new jail, there is 'Egg' island. It is uninhabited except for maybe some kind of wild life or birds or the occasional paddle boarder of kayaker who spends an overnight camping on it. The island is about five to ten acres in area and splattered out like a dropped egg. Crabtree himself had described it as an egg fallen from the heavens and thus it was 'Egg' Island to them. The east side of the island is at least ten feet above the surface of the Sound and the west side slopes down and disappears into the water.

The driver of the boat rammed its hull into the bank on the east side where it stuck. The three of them unloaded the body onto the sandy edge of the bank and one of them returned to the boat for a heavy piece of rope and several pieces of smaller ropes.

They struggled for several minutes to get the body over to the west side and then tied it securely to the heavy rope with some of the smaller ones. The driver stepped back from the body where the two women were still working, pulled a revolver with a silencer attached to it, called their names, and as they turned shot each of them in their foreheads. Twenty minutes later they were tied to the big heavy rope like the man who had called himself Levi Crabtree.

Apparently, someone knew that a large barge was approaching the Narrows, as the section of the Sound is called here and knew the pilot would have to almost stop to navigate around the Egg Island. With the heavy fog, he might have to bring the tug boat to a complete stop and wait until he could see.

Silt, sand and debris have to be dredged regularly too keep a channel open deep enough for the monstrous heavy barges to navigate through as the water has to be thirty to forty feet deep. In order to get past the island, the pilot must navigate an almost S turn to get around.

At this time the fog appeared to be lifting as hints of the sun were trying to break through from the east over at Destin. The barge did have to completely stop and the pilot didn't see the swimmer enter the cold black water dragging the heavy rope. The swimmer attached the rope to a huge hitch at the back of the tug, went under the water and resurfaced very near the island.

Finally the pilot took a chance of not grounding the barge and it started slowly on down the Sound. As it went, it drug the three bodies off the island. They made little splashing sounds as one, two, three they went into the dark, almost opaque black water. The barge slowly continued past the La Mancha complex, went under the bridge, and out into the bay dragging the three bodies behind it like fish on a stringer.

The swimmer started the boat to pull it lose from the bank, killed the engine, and let drift back down the Sound. It approached the house where it had picked up the two women with the body and glided into the lower level as a garage like door opened to let it in. The door lower causing little waves to circle out across the water as the driver climbed the stair which circled up one of the walls to the floor above.

The pick-up was missing from the drive down below. Everyone had done their jobs.

38

There is No Body

As I awoke the next morning in a room at Sacred Heart Hospital a nurse was doing what all nurses do—straightening my pillow, opening the drapes, and making sure the water glass was full. She exclaimed as she saw my eyes were opened, "And how are we this morning?"

I had the strongest urge to answer, "I sure as hell don't know about you but I hurt." But I didn't as I heard a voice say, "You better behave because she is the one with the needle."

I turned to the door and was surprised to see Daniel Sheraton standing there. Besides our visiting a few times and me being at the scene when he was bitten by the snake, I really didn't know Daniel. I just blurted out without thinking, "What are you doing here?"

He got a funny look on his face but replied, "Oh I just came by to see if you were still alive."

I thought that was strange but didn't have time to answer as Gladis came through the door. Gladis had brought a bunch of flowers and I immediately began to sneeze. The nurse took them out and Gladis looked embarrassed. I assured her it was okay.

She said, "You finally got it. Finally got hit by a car. I always thought a shark would jump out of the water and get you some morning when you were down there before dawn, but damn if it wasn't a car up on the Blvd. How bad you hurt?"

"I don't know. I just woke up and here you all are. So I guess I'm hurt pretty bad"

A doctor walked in and ask, "And just what do we have here? What are you two doing in here before visiting hours and before I see my patient? Leave right now."

As they did, I saw the back of Daniel's head and thought about what he had just said before Gladis interrupted.

I realized I was wrapped tightly around my chest and waist and found out that I had several cracked ribs. The doctor also told me that my right shoulder was dislocated when I arrived at the hospital. I also have several skinned bloody scrapes on both arms and legs.

There was no body. The deputies had searched all over the area behind Sea Shell building and found no evidence that anything at all had happened back there. There were no skid marks where the pick-up had crossed the median as it must have come across toward me on one of the paved crossovers. In fact, there was no pick-up that fit my description on the Island at all.

J C Blevins visited me the next morning, "Prof, you been working too hard going into that courtroom every morning and listening to them rattle on and on and then writing the day's happenings for the NorthWest Daily, and I think you are just worn out?"

"Maybe so, or I'm losing my mind, but I sure did get hit by that truck and I know I saw and heard an argument and a body fall from Sea Shell building."

"Well, I talked to everyone on the top three floors and they didn't hear anything that morning, so there's nothing I can do."

I laid in Scared Heart for three days wondering if I had lost my mind. I wondered how I would be able to attend court all wrapped up and hurting as I am, but I am determined to do it for I have become too involved.

169

39

No Eye Witnesses

The next morning my nurses after asking "How are we this morning?" and who knew who I was and that I wrote the events of the trial each day for the *NorthWest Daily*, brought the morning paper. I saw the byline and was proud that Julie Turri had been sent cover the court yesterday. She is a young go-getter whose personality exudes good feelings in anyone who is around. She's had been working with me and questioning me almost every day to make sure she understood what I had intended to write.

The headlines almost blared

EYE WITNESS TO DEATH OF VICTIM MISSING!

Good God, I thought as I began to read ▉▉▉ column.

During the trial yesterday as we sat listening to Judge Bickel reminding both attorneys to behave, Trooper J C Blevins entered the back of the courtroom and walked up to Prosecutor Porter's table. He leaned over and whispered something and Porter looked up at him in what I can only call disbelief.

Mr. Porter stood and asked Judge Bickel if he and Mr. Schaberg could approach the bench as he had something he wanted to share with them.

Judge Bickel called them forward where Mr. Porter leaned in and in a voice I could not hear, in fact almost whispered something to Judge Bickel and Mr. Schaberg.

But, the entire courtroom heard Judge Bickel's startled response, "What the Hell? What do you mean gone? I thought you had them secluded somewhere?"

"I thought so too, Your Honor."

Judge Bickel slammed his gavel on the little piece of hard wood on his bench and announced, "Court is in recess until further notice."

Just then Gladis came rushing into my hospital room, "Oh, I see you have seen the paper."

"I can't believe it. Tell me what happened."

"Well, your young friend got it just about right as far as I can see, except she may have missed one thing." She paused like she was getting her breath and I realized she was doing it on purpose—playing with my patience, "Alright, spill it."

"Well, after Bickel left the courtroom, Schaberg went back to his table and leaned over and told Launie the news, I guess, for she looked up at the courtroom and around until her eyes were on Ester Haynes, and God Almighty you should have seen that look. I'm sure glad Ester didn't look her way."

"Did you tell anyone else?"

"No."

"You've got to go find J C Blevins and tell him what you just told me. Ester Haynes is probably in a lot of danger.

"I didn't think of that," she said as she hurried out the door.

I sure wanted to get out of that bed and go home and when the doctor came, he said I could.

40

Ester is Missing

He thought he was going to be sick as he turned on the siren and sped down Highway 98 west until he came to the light for Memorial Drive. He served the car around several other cars and trucks that had partly pulled over to the side of the road and made a sweeping right turn onto Memorial.

He was probably breaking the speed limit by thirty miles as he looked for the sign for Pleasant Street. He had been to the house a couple of times; that morning when Ester Haynes hadn't shown up for court and another time when he persuaded her to let him take her and little Mitch to the Gulfarium Sealife Adventure Park.

He laughed to himself as he knew that she knew the trip was not for Mitch but for him to be with her. Mitch was far too you to know what was going on at the dolphin show but he had laughed as the dolphins leaped out of the water and dove down to come up yards away. Mitch had hugged his neck when Blevins handed him to Ester and she had turned red as she noticed it.

Now he couldn't even find Pleasant Street as he sped down Memorial. Finally there it was and he squealed into the street and spotted the little brown house. He pulled up in front of it and jumped out of the police car. He pounded on the door and Mrs. Kirk finally opened the door. "Grams, where's Ester and Mitch?" he almost shouted. She jumped back a little at his question and saw who it was as she said, "I haven't seen them since yesterday afternoon. Ester put Mitch in his stroller and they went down the sidewalk. I have no idea where they were going."

Blevins thought he would cuss as he thanked Mrs. Kirk and went back to his car realizing he had called the lady by the name all her grandkids did. He smiled and wonder what the nice lady thought. He could feel the morning coffee doing a number on his stomach but he sat for several minutes until an idea flashed into his mind.

He pulled away from the sidewalk, turned on the siren, made a turn in the street and sped back toward Memorial Drive. He looked both ways and saw no traffic and didn't even slow down as he screeched onto Memorial. A few blocks later he turned the car into the cemetery entrance, went down the lane to the group of tree, and there sat Ester on the bench. Little Mitch was playing on the grass near his father's grave.

Blevins jumped out of the car with the motor still running and raced to Ester. He grabbed her up off the bench and clutched her to him. She started to pull away but then relaxed and clung to him. Little Mitch looked up from the blanket she had spread out on the grass and stared at them.

Blevins told her what had happened to Sam and Alice and that he had no idea where to start looking for them, but that he was taking her and Mitch home to his house in Destin where they should be safe.

Ester pulled away from him and said, "J C, do you know what you are doing?"

"I'm going to get you two to a safe place."

"That's not what I mean and I think you know what I mean. You are a good and decent man, good looking even, but do you want to get involved with me? Me who can't get rid of the spirit of Mitch's dad. Me who thinks of nothing night and day but Ollie?"

"I think I might like to try…"

Ester smiled and gathered up Mitch and his things and headed for the patrol car. Mitch had ridden in it before and said, "Whoooeee!"

Blevins and Ester turned and smiled at each other. He turned on the siren as they went down Memorial toward Highway 98 and little Mitch was shouting as loud as he could, "Whoooeee!"

41

A Matter of Convenience

Bay Shore Drive is about as big an oxymoron as the house on Tarpon Street on the Island. It curves along the shore of Choctawhatchee Bay lined with ancient Life Oak trees many of which have joined branches creating a tunnel sometimes for blocks. Spanish Moss is draped like shreds of cotton candy on almost every tree. Faulkner would feel right at home here but he wouldn't call the moss cotton candy but something much more sinister or morose. The houses on the Bay side are large relatively new mansions on lots that are an acre or larger. Bicycle Bob's family lived on Brooks Street which mingles with Bay Shore Drive for several blocks before it turns off to the right—right up to the Bay.

As I drive along on my way to meet Bob at his boat on what he insists is 'Good Thing Lake' which I'm quite sure he and his buddies made up during high school for it is nowhere on any of the maps I've looked at—it's labeled Lake Earl on the maps, I pass the house where Bob spent his young years which is still occupied by the family who bought it from Bob's parents. It sets way back from the street right at the edge of the Bay and he told me it has nine bedrooms and his mother never knew which one he would spend the night in—seems it was a running joke at his house. The yard is filled with Life Oaks and Magnolia trees.

But the puzzle is that across the street the houses are low concrete block houses one story tall which were built in the 1940's or '50's. They were built to withstand high winds and have several times been bombarded with hurricane strong winds. They look meager—almost ghetto-like— compared to the other side of the street. I pass the corner of Gardner and Bay Shore Drive where Michael Duluca lives with his wife Tia. Their house is much the same as their neighbor's except Tia keeps a meticulous lawn which is filled with so many shrubs and tropical plants that you barely notice the house.

Sometime in the fifties someone with a lot of money started to redevelop the neighborhood but the only thing completed was a long channel cut from Good Thing Lake that runs for several blocks south to right behind Michael's house so Michael and Paul, his partner, look after Bob's fishing boat. Bob's is not the only boat on the channel as Judge Bickel has his much bigger speed boat hanging in dry dock within view of where Bob docks *The Choctaw Pride*, his twenty-nine foot Ocean 290 Super Sport. The Judge seldom uses his yacht and Bob cusses it every time he takes his boat out to fish or sight-see around the area, "The Son of a Bitch just has it there to get my goat. The lousy fucker."

I have to drive on a few blocks so I can turn up the unnamed lane which runs alongside the channel. Bay Shore Drive turns into Yacht Club Parkway before I get to my turn and I must pass Judge Bickel's house which dominates this street as he prides himself that it is the largest estate in town. Bob swears, "The bastard only bought that place to show me up. Hell, it's only three blocks from the Yacht Club that my dad helped establish and old Squeeze Box is getting his jollies off showing off his money to me."

Bob isn't at his little dock and *The Choctaw Pride* is in its slip. I let my cell phone ring his number several times and remember he has never set-up his phone to answer calls. I get into Annabelle, my Four Runner, and head back down the lane to Bay Shore Drive.

*

We see Michael and Paul around the La Mancha almost every day for they modernize condos and this summer there seem to be many that are being remodeled. They drive a nondescript converted an old cross country rental truck that they turned into a workshop. This really has been a remarkable summer for them as the La Mancha has as many as five condos to renovate at one time, so they have worked late into the nights. Paul is a very likable young man in his early thirties who is 'mute.' There's nothing wrong with his hearing, but he was born unable to speak.

Each of the six buildings at the La Mancha have 'closets' at the end of each floor which are just single rooms that are in great demand as storage units to the owners of condos. Somehow, Michael has convinced Bette that he should be able to use at least one of those rooms in each building, so we see Paul carrying box after box of building materials to those rooms. Since they are not allowed to begin construction work in the mornings until 9 o'clock because of the noise he and Paul always make with their saws and the hammering, they usually work late in the evenings on jobs which don't make noise like laying floor tile or painting rooms. I've seen Paul many evenings carrying boxes of floor tiles from one of the storage closets to some condo.

Paul is a hundred percent British, very good looking, and 'strong as a mule' as my granddad use to say of someone who is all buffed up from working so hard and taking care of himself.

The La Mancha has had a very busy summer, much more than last season—maybe because of all the horrible happenings of last year—and the Condo Association is very happy with the work Bette is doing. At the Association meeting this morning she reported the surprising upturn in business and also announced the upgrading that Michael and Paul are doing and that they would be working late into the fall even after the Snow Birders arrive.

Shirley Herd, who always questions anything unusual that is happing around the La Mancha asked, "Why are we getting so many short stays this year? It seems to me that we have people coming in one night and leaving two nights later. There also seems to be a lot fewer families who come and stay a week or longer. I heard that a family who has been coming to the La Mancha for many years couldn't get a reservation for their two week vacation."

Bette's answer met with the approval of most present when she said, "The sluggish economy around the Country might have something to do with it but in a way it is good for it keeps our cleaning crews busier for the condos need to be cleaned more often."

Shirley is used to having the last word on a matter and she replied, "Heaven help us if the people who do come hear about the rattlesnake and spread the word that it might still be here."

"I think we can be very safe in saying that the snake is long gone. No one has seen it for weeks and I'm thinking that mysterious cat killed and ate if before it died of the snake bites," Bette replied and then hurried on to another topic that the General in charge at Eglin had agreed to help pay to replace the broken down fence that separates the La Mancha from the Air Command. I saw a look of relief come over her face as almost everyone present approved with many positive comments and the meeting was over.

"By the way, has anyone seen Bob the last couple of days? He usually comes up to see me every morning but he hasn't been around. And he certainly never misses this meeting which he would have conducted."

There were several comments among those at the meeting with comments that Bob hadn't been around but no one seemed to know why or where he might be.

I walked out of the meeting with Bette and she asked about the trial and would it ever end? I assured her that it would end but no one knew how or when. We bumped into Paul in the hallway and Bette asked, "Have you seen Bob this week?" He shook his head that he hadn't and we walked on until we reached the stairs up to her office and I went on my way to the Pelican.

I'm one of the few at the La Mancha who knows Bette will return to her office which looks out over the guard shack and is in sight of the house on Tarpon Street and then Brooks Bridge in the distance, and take an excellent bottle of Scotch out of her desk drawer, pour herself a glass half full, and sit sipping it satisfied she has please the condo owners.

42

Faithful

Paul drove the old rental van too fast down Bay Shore Drive, up the sandy lane that is lined with the boat docks and slammed on the brakes as he reached Bob's dock. He had taken care of *The Choctaw Pride* for over a year making sure it was ready each Wednesday for Bob's weekly fishing trips. By this time he had about as much pride in the sleek fishing boat as Bob did and he enjoyed making Bob proud of it. Bob paid him way too much money to take care of the boat and Paul had tried to convey that to him many times, but Bob would just laugh as he boarded the boat to steer it down the canal, across the Bay down to Destin Pass, and out into the Gulf.

He honked the horn thinking perhaps Bob was asleep below deck but Tia DuLuca appeared in her back yard and after shouting what did he want, it took Paul a minute or so to pantomime Bob to her—he held his arms way out from his body, wobbled back and forth, and then held imaginary handlebars what wobbled in his hands. Tia laughed aloud, shook her head, hollered that she had not seen Bob, and went back into her house.

He stepped down onto the dock, saw that no one had disturbed the boat for he knew just how he had left it, and reached over to hold the heavy reinforcement bar that they tied the boat to. He looked down into the sandy debris cover bottom where he knew Bob had hidden a heavy metal chest. Bob had told him of the chest and Paul had never bothered it.

He got back into the van and headed back to cross Brooks Bridge and go down Santa Rosa Blvd to the La Mancha. As he past Tarpon Street he slowed down and almost turned into the drive but went on to the guard house and into the La Mancha. For several minutes he was bothered thinking about the house on Tarpon, so he stopped painting a door facing, grabbed Michael and pulled him to come with him. They went outside, got in the van, and headed to Tarpon Street.

43

Daniel and His Cabin

Daniel Sheraton had been the starting catcher for the Choctaw High baseball team as a junior and during his senior year and it's well known that catchers have to have strong durable legs. The muscles in Daniel's thighs corded in hard thick ropes whenever he was lifting eight or ten of those heavy beach chairs to carry them out to be set-up for guests.

As he drove his old blue Nissan toward Blackwater River State Park to repair some things on the little cabin he had bought three months ago as a surprise for Lyn, he tightened the muscles in his legs and stretched. He was sore and weakened by the snake bite on his left ankle and the three days he had to spend in Sacred Heart Hospital while the doctors had shot him with antivenin to make sure the rattler's poison was out of his system.

He had taken Lyn to the same hospital two nights ago as she had started labor with Dylan and she was still there. He thought maybe he should turn around and go back to Fort Walton Beach to be close to her, but he wanted so much to have the little cabin ready when the baby came and thought maybe they could spend Thanksgiving there with their new son. And besides, Lyn was a nurse and everyone at the hospital knew and respected her.

So he drove on. Lyn's smile flashed through his mind and he remembered that was what had attracted him to her in the first place. He was already past Crestview and had been on Interstate 10 for a few miles. When he came to the Holt exit, he made a right turn and followed the outer road until he came to Highway 90 where he turned north for the last few miles to the park.

He worked for three hours or more repairing a place on the roof and the screen on the porch which ran across the front of the cabin. He was very pleased with himself and had a great big urge to tell Lyn about it, but he thought he could wait until she had the baby and he could drive them up and surprise her with it.

He headed back along the swift moving water of the river, past the tumbling falls that everyone admires so much, and spooked a Brown Bear at the sound of his car. He watched as it went lumbering into the undergrowth on the other side of the river carrying a large fish in its mouth and looking back at him with nearly every step it took. He smiled contentedly as he realized his little cabin was on land that butted up against the park land and he would be able to fish to his content in years to come.

He would teach Dylan to respect and love this forest as he did, he hoped. He wanted to teach him that the river got its color from so much dark tannic water; that "Blackwater" is a translation of the Choctaw's word *oka-lusa*, which means "water black."

He imagined standing with him at the base of that huge white cedar that was called a Florida Champion in 1982. He wondered how old that tree was.

He wanted Dylan to see all the animals he had come to love and to learn about them and know how to treat them; the white-tailed deer that threw up their flags as they ran away, the turkeys and how you could so easily trick them in coming at your 'turkey call,' the cautious and dangerous bobcats.

He remembered the enormous gator he encountered one day on a white sand bar. So many of the animals he had learned as a kid were up here like those silly playful otters he had hidden from and watched all morning one day. And the birds: red-headed and pileated woodpeckers, hawks, crows, warblers and Mississippi kites, plovers and sandpipers, and his favorite—those sneaky and sharp-eyed herons.

He loved the outdoors, always had since as a little kid he had wondered the Ranger Woods on Eglin when his dad was stationed there.

He was relishing all these things that he had grown to love as he passed a little road that turned off to the right and he noticed that it had been used recently. Usually the little lane was grown up with high patches of wiregrass and sticky saw palmetto and sometimes fallen limbs of trees which lined both sides of the lane looked like they had blocked it but they had all been flattened out almost to the wet ground. There had been a heavy rain a few days ago and Daniel could clearly see that a car had been down the lane but the tracks only made one trip, so either the car was still down there or something was wrong.

Normally he thought he would have gone on by, but something made him turn around and turn into the little lane. He went about a half mile and up ahead of him, he saw the old building which looked like a tool shed that contractors might have left after they had built so many buildings just inside the park.

He stopped and got out of his car and walked to the door of the shed. He was surprised to see a rusty old chain hung through the two handles and what looked like a new lock locking the two ends together.

He shouted, "Hello?" and was startled as two voices began hollering inside the building.

A few minutes later after Daniel smashed the handle from one side of the door with a hammer from his car, Sam Ripley stood holding Alice Pearl in his arms in front of him. Alice, sobbing historically was trying to cover herself as they both were in nothing but their underwear.

Sam's first words were, "You got any food? We've been here for days and Alice is really weak."

"Just some crackers. How about water?"

As he hurried back to the cars to get the box of crackers he had munched on driving from home, Sam called after him, "We got water that leaked through the ceiling from the rain."

He returned with the crackers and a piece of painter's cloth he had brought along as he had done some painting in the cabin. He handed them both to Sam who wrapped the cloth around Alice and started feeding her some of the crackers. She wanted to gulp them down but he made her eat them slowly as he held her up against his chest.

It only took a minute for Sam to tell Daniel who they were and why they had been locked in the shed. Sam asked, "Do you have a phone with you?"

"Man, doesn't everyone? I couldn't come up here and not have it because I'm going to be a daddy and need to keep in touch."

"Neat! Can I use it to call J C Blevins? I know his number by heart since we have talked so many times this summer and fall."

"Sure," he pulled the phone from his pocket.

Sam punched in the numbers and in a couple of minutes had filled Blevins in on what had happened. Blevins was shouting with disbelief and wanted to talk with Daniel.

"Yes? Sure I know who you are. I've been following this murder trial like everyone else in the county. Besides, you talked to me last summer at the La Mancha. Yeah, sure do. I'll bring them there to you. I don't think anyone has any idea that they are free. I haven't seen anyone paying attention, but we are barely back out on the road. By the way, there's an old pick-up parked behind that little shed which fits the description of the one Prof said hit him. We're on our way. Should be there in an hour."

Sam Ripley sitting in the front seat in his boxers reached over and took Alice Pearl's hand as she huddled in the back seat. Their eyes met and they didn't have to say they loved each other nor did they have to say how lucky they felt.

And then one of those moments happened, one that isn't planned and might never happen again to the people who experience it as they said nearly in perfect unison, "Thanks, Daniel, we're going to name our first born after you."

Everyone laughed and Daniel's little blue car sped off toward Fort Walton Beach.

He delivered them to J C Blevins who swore him to secrecy about them being free and back in Fort Walton Beach. As both of them were really on their own with no relatives in the area J C took them to jail where he locked them into a cell on the third floor.

Daniel's cell phone rang and a nurse at the hospital told him Lyn was having the baby. He sped through the streets but he was scrubbed down and in the room when Dylan Sheraton came into the world.

Daniel leaned over and kissed Lyn's forehead. He looked down at her and that smile melted his heart. Over at one side of the room where they were washing him, Dylan was announcing to the world with all his seven energetic pounds that he had good lungs.

44

It's Over

The next day Judge Bickel reconvened court.

Schaberg request a meeting at his bench with Porter and Bickel allowed it.

"Your Honor, my client is not getting a fair trial. How in the world do you or anyone else expect this jury to be able to remember what has happened in the courtroom with the numerous recesses we have had. Besides that, they have been secluded in some motel or resort somewhere and have been away from their families, work, and friends, whatever. Therefore the Defense is asking for a mistrial in this case. I have prepared the papers and will file them with you this afternoon."

Porter interjected, "Your Honor, part of the Prosecution's stand on this matter agrees with Mr. Schaberg but I would remind the court that it is not the Prosecution's fault that these proceedings have been going on so long."

I would say again, "Bull Shit, sir. You have dallied around with witnesses like Ester Haynes which really had no bearing on the murder trial. You lost your two eye witnesses to what you are claiming was murder. So, how can you say that the Prosecution is not responsible?"

"I would remind the Judge that many of the recesses were call by himself. I would remind him also that he could not control the crowded courtroom and that he took personal time to be away from the trial."

"Mr. Porter, you are close to being held in contempt."

"I respectfully ask that we try to proceed and I will start my summation if that is your ruling."

"Agreed. Mr. Schaberg, will you agree to going right to the summation?'

Schaberg looked like he had won the lottery as he answered, "Gladly, Your Honor."

Judge Bickel could not believe that Porter had just conceded, or almost conceded, the case. It was eleven o'clock and he decided that court would resume after lunch.

"Ladies and Gentlemen of the Jury, we have decided to resume the trial right after lunch today. Court is now once again in recess until after lunch."

There were groans from all corners of the courtroom and I saw some looks of total disbelief on the faces of several jurors, but as Bickel left the courtroom the jury was also dismissed so Katrina Hart could take them to lunch.

I saw J C Blevins rush through the back door of the courtroom and go quickly to Mr. Porter's table. He leaned in and Porter looked shocked and then he smiled. Now all he had to do is get out of what he had agreed about summary statements for Blevins had Sam Ripley and Alice Pearl in a cell upstairs in the jail.

Forty-five minutes later when court was called to order, Porter and Schaberg stood before Judge Bickel's bench.

"Your Honor, I would like to amend what I agreed about this morning. I would like to call two eye-witnesses to the stand." He had broken the rules of a meeting at the bench for he said the last part loud enough for the whole courtroom to hear it.

Schaberg looked like he had been shot as he almost stuttered, "Your Honor, I strongly object. Mr. Porter agreed this morning that we would start our summations and the Defense has worked through lunch making ready to present his."

Bickel did something that Porter would never forget until he realized what Bickel said was just for show, "Mr. Schaberg, the public and Okaloosa County would never again agree with anything I did. I would be the laughing stock of the whole county. My courtroom would never again be the place where the important trials of the day would be held. So, I am letting Mr. Porter proceed in calling his two witnesses."

Schaberg look at Bickel like he had just signed both their death certificates; he looked sick, very sick, as he had turned extremely pale. He requested a very short recess so he could go to the restroom.

Bickel allowed it.

"Ladies and Gentlemen of the Jury and members of the court, we will recess for ten minutes for Mr. Schaberg to go to the restroom."

There were groans first and then fits of laughter.

I saw Blevins talking with Porter and then he walked out the door of the courtroom on his way upstairs, I assumed, to get Sam Ripley and Alice Pearl and escort them down to the court.

If Bicycle Bob had been sitting next to me, I would have a very sore leg. I am worried about Bob for no one has seen him for several days. Something is wrong for I don't think he would take off somewhere without telling me. I guess it's just the old man thinking the worst again.

Schaberg leaned in and obviously told Launie that the two witnesses were upstairs and that they would be testifying. He walked quickly to the rear door of the courtroom and left.

Launie was stunned. Her face was filled with rage as she jumped to her feet cussing and headed straight for Judge Bickel.

Katrina Hart stepped in front of her, raised her gun and shot Launie right between the eyes, "It's over Bitch." A faint look of disbelieve cross Launie's face as blood gushed from the little hole in her forehead. As she crumbled to the floor her body lodged against the Defense table; she slid down one of the legs of the table and landed sitting upright blankly staring out at the courtroom.

The courtroom was in total silence until the shock of what had just happened enveloped them for this time Katrina Hart's revolver did not have a silencer on it and the loud explosion had startled all of us. The gruesome figure of Launie sitting there with that vacant stare of death caused the people in the room to almost stampede to the back door. Above it all I heard Ester Haynes scream, "It's done, Ollie, it's done." The jury started as a group toward the backroom where they always entered but saw that Katrina blocked it, so they turned as one person and headed for the back door where they crushed up against all the other people trying to get out. There was pandemonium as everyone in the courtroom tried to exit there.

Katrina shouted above the roar, "Either stop or be shot. I will start killing the ones closest to me and continue as long as I have ammunition." People stopped where they were. During all the confusion she had made her way up to Judge Bickel's chair, she walked around behind him, encircled his neck with her arm, held the gun to his temple and ordered him to stand. She hollered, "I have Judge Bickel and will shoot him as easily as I have Launie if anyone tries to stop us from leaving." She pulled Bickel through the door behind his bench and barricaded the door with a chair under the door knob.

Porter sat at his table in shock.

The killing of Launie Sanderson and the confusion after the shot took only a few minutes, but Schaberg had been very busy as it was happening. He had run from the courthouse down to the Landing where the *Lollipop* had been anchored since Launie's arrest. He started the big powerful engines and had it ready to leave.

I hurried to a window that looked out toward the Landing behind the courthouse and saw Katrina Hart and Judge Bickel exit the outside door and hop into the golf cart that was waiting there. They sped down the sidewalk and jumped aboard the *Lollipop*. Schaberg pulled the big yacht away from the dock and headed out into the Sound.

45

Steak and White Russians

"Damn it to Hell, that's not how this was supposed to work," Bob had growled as he first became aware of where he was five days ago.

He had been sitting on his balcony with a pitcher of White Russians and a huge rib steak was sizzling away on the grill as he was getting ready to watch three NFL games from the three big flat screens that crowd his condo's living room.

The Prof had persuaded him to switch from sirloins to rib steaks a few weeks ago and he didn't give a damn that he ate about three of them a week. "Screw em all," he bellowed, "I'll do as I damn well please." His enjoyment was NFL, steaks, and White Russians; a little graduation from his remembered high school days which were football, women, and marijuana. He laughed.

He thought about the mistakes he made after high school when he decided no college unlike that son of a bitch Bickel did. His almost fatal wreck, the biggest mistake he ever made raced through his head as the pain and fear he had filled his mind. "What a dumb ass I am," he thought.

The steak was off the grill and resting when the phone rang and she said he was wanted at the house right away. He let out his usual, "Damn it to Hell," put the steak in the oven with the veggies that were roasted, went down and got his bicycle, and peddled over to Tarpon Drive.

He barely touched the button on the elevator when the door opened. He pushed his bicycle in and crowded his way in with it and punched the 'up' button. When the door opened at the floor above, she greeted him with

"The boss will be here in about thirty minutes, but in the meantime I've made your usual."

He felt the cool glass and tasted the refreshing drink and thought she sure knew how he liked them. Fifteen minutes later he was out cold.

A long time must have passed for when he came to he was very hungry and thirsty. He felt the pain first and then looked down at his right ankle; it was raw and caked with dried blood and rivers of fresh blood ran through the caked blood where the leg cuff rubbed it raw. It was attached to a thick heavy rope that encircled a bar in the window that faces the Sound in the direction of Brooks Bridge. Like it was meant to torment him, the rope had been tied with a sailor's knot that he knew he could never reach to untie.

Someone must have been in the room recently and he must have dozed off for a fresh pitcher of White Russians and a steaming steak sat on the table just out of his reach. He cussed and stretched as far as he could to reach the table about six feet in front of him but it was just out of his grasp.

Rivulets of condensation ran down the pitcher's icy sides and he let out another stream of cussing. A fork jabbed straight up into the thick steak had released a puddle of juice surrounding the steak on the plate.

Then he really let out a streak of cussing as he saw a beautiful white cloth napkin was folded neatly beside the plate and he realized it was one of his mother's napkins he proudly used when he had people over at his condo. He tugged and yanked on the rope in swift jerks as he tried to free himself but the bar in the window was too much for him.

He slammed his fist against tabletop again and again until he saw blood running from the gashes where it scraped raw. He saw on tiny window was open and through it he saw the Sound and Brooks Bridge and he began yelling through it until he realized he was must yelling out into the dark waters of the Sound.

A day that had haunted all his life popped into his mind; he was eleven and his Dad had said, "If you're going to amount to anything, which I doubt, then you better be the best at something and that's my joke for the day." Well, he had been the best; he could catch and run with a football better than his old man ever thought about, he had girls swarming all over his strong young body because he was the best on the field, and he made more friends than his old man ever imagined because he was able to take care of his buddies with the very best marijuana around. Now he was losing the game, his pants were not big enough and he knew it and he heard his Dad laughing.

"Damn it to Hell," he spit, "Why was I crazy enough to get into this insane contest?" He had enough money and anything else he wanted but he wasn't about to be bested again. That idiot Crabtree was supposed to be just a diversion to keep the Prof and others at the La Mancha off guard about what was really happening at Launie Sanderson's trial. That son of a bitch and that bitch of a woman with him had killed Walkin Al in a way that no man should die and just because she suspected Al recognized her from the days she worked at Luanie's place. Damn it, he had like Al and he could not erase from his mind the look on Al's face as the snake lunged into his neck.

He hadn't intended to push Crabtree off his balcony when he had called him over to talk about Al's death but they got into a big argument and he had shoved Crabtree backwards and then reached out and twisted his neck until he heard that sickening snap and as Crabtree fell over the balcony. He knew the pick-up was down by the Blvd but had no idea what those two other strippers had done with Crabtree's body and had spent two or three days in fear that J C Blevins would find some kind of evidence down on the lawn in front of his balcony that a body had landed there. He breathed a lot easier when J C was called off somewhere else.

194

Then Daniel Sheraton had seen one of the beach's paddle boards floating down the Sound with that stupid bitch, Eva, strapped to it. Serves her right for what she did to Al, but he had no idea who had done that for he thought she had been sent back down to Miami to get her out of Fort Walton Beach. There must have two of them that strapped her to that board for he didn't think one person could strap her to the board like that—so Crabtree and who else, he wondered. He heard that Daniel saw the board floating down the Sound up-side-down and just barely above the water.

He knew there would be Hell to pay when the big boss found out that the whole plan had been fucked up so bad, so that was the reason he had been chained up for the last five days he thought. He was the scapegoat. He was going to pay.

He was paying. He was so thirsty his mouth tasted like chalk and his stomach continuously rumbled with hunger.

Why had he been involved with Launie Sanderson since she came to Fort Walton Beach? He could only think of one answer—he just wanted to show them all what a big shot he could be pulling strings. Oh, the money had filled his bank account, but he didn't care as he already had plenty.

Now, "Fuck the whole bunch and the bicycle they rode in on," he thought as he let go of one of his bellowing laughs.

He had been chained up for five days he knew and had nothing to eat the whole time. He had finally pissed out all the White Russians as his urine ran down his legs but he was starving and felt like a knife cut through it every time he swallowed.

He heard the door to the Sound squeal open and knew someone had entered the room down below. He heard the door rumble down closed again and he sat waiting looking at the hole where the stairs came up into the room he was in but nobody appeared. He yelled and yelled but realized he couldn't yell loud enough for whoever it was to hear him and then he thought that maybe he didn't want to be heard by whoever it was.

He smelled the smoke before he heard the explosion of the boat fuel down in the lower level of the house and soon the smoke was billowing up out of the open stairwell opening down into that room. He heard the crackle of the burning and after giving the rope one more tremendous jerk, he sat calmly in his chair waiting.

He laughed aloud as he thought he wouldn't have to worry like he always did since Launie came because no one knew he was the one who got her the licenses to open her business. He wouldn't have to face the humiliation of what he had done.

"Dumb Ass," he thought as he tried to imagine why he had got caught up in this whole fucking mess. Just to prove he was better than someone else? He realized his mind was going in circles and he wondered what others would say about him after they found out. That was the only concern he had as the smoke got thicker and the heat in the room caused rivulets of sweat to run down his big jaws like the condensation on that pitcher just out of his reach.

As he looked through the window—one of those freaky Gothic windows along the east side of the room---he saw the *Lollipop* speeding up the Sound to go under Brooks Bridge and escape into Choctawhatchee Bay.

He laughed that loud boisterous laugh of his one more time for he knew what was about to happen.

46

The Best Laid Plans are Often Screwed

Schaberg steered the big blue and white yacht carefully down the Sound keeping it in the deep water the barges used. He kept glancing back toward the County Jail expecting water patrol boats to come speeding out from the dock underneath the building, but he didn't see any and he knew he couldn't go any faster. He was unfamiliar with the *Lollipop* and didn't know where the barge channel was so he had to watch for the buoys and so they were going down the Sound very slowly.

The calculating little lawyer started thinking to himself, "Is this really going to work? Are we going to pull this off?" The answer was no, of course, he realized because even if they got all the way back to Miami someone would be coming after them. He knew also that since they had messed up things so much that Katrina's dad would get rid of them anyway. He wondered what her dad would do to Judge Bickel. Would his wife Diana be able to talk her dad out of killing him for the sake of their seven kids—his grandkids?

And then, Schaberg decided he just didn't care. He was never going to go back to Miami. He was going to get off this boat somewhere between here and there and disappear for good.

Katrina Hart walked up just then and stood beside him. As he turned toward her she said, "Schaberg you played your part. You did a great job of being the idiot you are in the courtroom, but we don't have any more use for you."

She held the gun in her hand up to his forehead and shot him. The silencer had muffled the sound so she had no concern that anyone had heard it. She turned to Judge Bickel and said, "Well, I have no more use for this," as she threw the gun over into the black water of the Sound. "And we'll dispose of this when we get out into the Gulf down past Destin" as she stepped over Schaberg's body and reached for the steering wheel.

Bickel smiled at her and walked to her and wrapped his arms around her as she faced away from him cupping her breasts in his hands, "We made a good pair in that court, didn't we? Let's see if we can continue this. Let's not go to Miami. Let's just go off and get lost somewhere."

She looked up at him and smiled, "I thought you wouldn't ask me." They both laughed and he leaned to kiss her neck.

Either Crabtree had set the timer on the bomb wrong or Bob had told him wrong for the explosion rocked the Sound from the jail to Brooks Bridge. The Narrows shook with the reverberations for several minutes. Bits of the *Lollipop* blew so high that they fell on the roadway that goes across the bridge. The big tanks Launie had installed in the yacht so it could travel a long distance had been full when Crabtree had attached the timing devise to the engine of the big blue and white yacht.

"Damn it to hell," Bob cussed as he saw the flying debris of the *Lollipop* as it careened about the two shores of the Sound smashing into windows that shattered into sailing missiles, "that wasn't supposed to happen until it was past the bridge and way out into the Bay." He heard the crash of cars smashing into each other and into buildings along Main Street. He imagined bits of Judge Bickel splatting down into the dark water of the Sound to become catfish food. He laughed aloud and it sounded almost like the 'Haw! Haw! Haw!' of the crows.

A second latter his laugh changed from the bitter almost yell of fear and hatred to an amazement that became Bob's usual loud boisterous sincere happy laugh.

47

Uh-Oh

A week had past. She had sat in her big leather chair and watched the house on Tarpon Drive crumble into a jagged mess of tangled beams. She had heard the fire engines as they came blaring down Santa Rosa Blvd and almost laughed as she imagined the firemen's faces when they realized there was no door knob on the outside of the house. She had watched as they hurried around the house and then had returned and seemed to be standing watching the house burn. She had seen smoke coming from one of the lower windows and thought maybe it had exploded and the smoke was escaping through the empty hole.

She had watched with an amused expression as she first heard and then felt the massive explosion of the *Lollipop* as it rattled the windows of her office that overlooks the lawn of the La Mancha. That had settled a big problem for her, she realized as she was certain that Bickel, Hart, and Schaberg were dead.

She had called Miami yesterday to report the loss of the yacht, that Bicycle Bob was burned in the fire, and that she would have to get someone else to go out into the Gulf to pick up deliveries.

The glass of expensive Scotch shattered on the hardwood floor below when he asked, "What do you mean you have to get someone to replace Bob? Someone picked up that double shipment you asked for— picked it up yesterday at the usual drop place."

Edwards Brothers Malloy
Thorofare, NJ USA
February 9, 2016